boy proof

Cecil Castellucci

CANDLEWICK PRESS
CAMBRIDGE, MASSACHUSETTS

To all nerdy girls everywhere

Copyright © 2005 by Cecil Castellucci

First paperback edition 2006

The Library of Congress has cataloged the hardcover edition as follows:

Castellucci, Cecil, date.
Boy proof / Cecil Castellucci. —1st U.S. ed.
p.   cm.
Summary: Feeling alienated from everyone around her, Los Angeles high school senior and cinephile Victoria Jurgen hides behind the identity of a favorite movie character until an interesting new boy arrives at school and helps her realize that there is more to life than just the movies.
ISBN-10 0-7636-2333-4 (hardcover)
ISBN-13 978-0-7636-2333-3 (hardcover)
[1. Identity—Fiction. 2. Motion picture industry—Fiction. 3. Motion pictures—Fiction. 4. High schools—Fiction. 5. Schools—Fiction. 6. Interpersonal relations—Fiction. 7. Los Angeles (Calif.)—Fiction.] I. Title.

PZ7.C26865Bo 2005
[Fic]—dc22   2004050256

ISBN-10 0-7636-2796-8 (paperback)
ISBN-13 978-0-7636-2796-6 (paperback)

10 9 8 7 6 5 4 3 2 1

Printed in the United States of America

This book was typeset in Sabon.

Candlewick Press
2067 Massachusetts Avenue
Cambridge, Massachusetts 02140

visit us at www.candlewick.com

For supporting me and my arty ways, I'd like to acknowledge my family—Lise, Vincent, and Laurent Castellucci; my most excellent friends—you rule most mightily, especially those who bought me a latte, lent me $100, or drove me somewhere; my agent, Barry "Mr. Fantastic" Goldblatt; SCBWI-LA Working Writers Retreat, Kerry Slattery and Skylight Books in Los Feliz, Margot Gerber and American Cinematheque, The Banff Centre Writing with Style Program, Andrea Kleine, Phil Glau, Collyn Justus, Carolyn Kellogg, Tim Wynne-Jones, Tom Burman at the Burman Studio, the Tuesday Night Writers Group (R.I.P.), The Alpha 60 Filmmaking Club, and Liz Bicknell at Candlewick; special thanks to my editor, the divine Kara "Kick-Ass" LaReau; and a very special thanks to Steve Salardino for suggesting I write a book called *Boy Proof*.

Monday. January 5. 6:59 A.M.
Cyberspace.

REUTERS: DOOMSDAY CLOCK MOVES CLOSER TO MIDNIGHT
A.P.: DOUBT AND SHOCK GREET FIRST HUMAN CLONING
SPACE.COM: ASTEROID ON COLLISION COURSE WITH EARTH
SCIENCE: SIXTH MASS EXTINCTION HAS BEGUN

"Great, another stellar day," I say.

I flick off my computer and head for school.

When I arrive, as per usual, I don't acknowledge a single soul.

I don't say, "Hello, Rue."

"Hello, Martin."

"Hello, Hasan."

"Hello, Nelly."

"Hello, Inez."

"Hello, Katrina."

"Hello, Damon."

"Hello, Ignacio."

And no one says hello to me all day. But I don't care.

Last period, I book for Mrs. Perez's AP English class, making it in just as the bell rings. There is something new today that I don't like at all. A new kid is sitting next to me.

I slide into my seat, scanning him with my laser-sharp modified eyes. I notice a smell. It's skunky, musky, boy sweat. For a second I think I like it. Then I decide it's gross.

He stinks, I think. *The new boy stinks.*

I move away from him and then look at him sideways. Why did Mrs. Perez have to sit him next to me? It is so unfair.

I look at him again. His hair is black and slicked back into a small ponytail. There are flakes of dandruff on his black sweatshirt. He is wearing black jeans and a black T-shirt that says *Hellblazer.* That seems to be the coolest thing about him. I like that comic book.

I shift away from him.

He is working on his environmental poem, scratching away like a chicken. I can see by the crinkle in his brow that he is struggling with it. He's probably not that smart.

"What are you looking at?" he whispers, turning to look at me.

He has nice eyes, the new kid, even though the rest of him is disgusting.

2

"I'm not looking. I'm smelling," I say, putting on my best Egg impression. When I have to speak to strangers, I turn into her.

"Let's make a rule," I add. "If you sit here, you have to shower."

By reading his face I can tell he expected something different to come out of my mouth. Instead of being shocked, his face cracks into a movie-star antihero smile.

"I just got off an airplane. I've got travel slime," he explains.

He looks me over. His pretty eyes look me up and down, taking in my shaved head, my ring-covered ears, my colored-in eyebrows, my pale skin.

I make my most scary face. The one where I bulge my eyes out like I'm dead.

"Boo!" I spit at him.

"Whoa!" He puts his hands up in mock surrender and then goes back to working on his poem.

"Impressive, it took you thirty seconds to cringe. That's the longest anyone's gone ever."

"Well, I'm a winner," he says.

I look up at the clock. It's two-twenty. I watch the second hand inch by the face. I concentrate on it and try to bend time like Egg does in *Terminal Earth*. No such luck. Time won't move any faster for me.

I've been done with my poem for twenty minutes. I

can slip out of school early. There's a three-thirty show-ing of *Terminal Earth,* which is only the best movie ever made, starring Zach Cross as Uno and Saba Greer as Egg.

I grab my army bag and shove my seat into place with a bang and head out the back door of the class-room.

"See you later," the new kid says as I push past him.

"Not likely," I say.

And then he chuckles.

Asshole.

3:07 P.M.

Two-Dollar Movie Theater.

I shove the rest of a bagel in my mouth as I go to snag my perfect seat in the movie theater, fifth row from the front, exactly center screen. The theater is dilapidated, frayed at the edges, stale smelling. The curtain, once magnificent, looks like a sad garbage bag.

But I can see through the wear and tear of time. I can imagine the theater in its glory days, when it was new and bright. When there was a piano on that stage. When Buster Keaton and Charlie Chaplin had swank film pre-mieres. When there were women in beaded dresses and beaded shoes. When men wore suits and hats were in fashion.

Sometimes, though, it's harder to picture.

I heard from the concession-stand guy that the theater has been sold. That means no more two-dollar first-run movies by this time next year. That's not necessarily a bad thing, except that I wonder if they are going to reupholster the seats. I like the theater the way it is, all worn and frayed, hinting at its greater glory. They'll ruin it by making it modern, by adding cup holders to the seats and some bacteria-resistant carpet. I wonder if they're going to charge fourteen dollars and serve sushi. That would be annoying.

Terminal Earth, my favorite movie, has three screenings left today, and I plan on staying for them all. They say the DVD isn't going to come out until the summer. I hate having to wait for it. My "friend" on the *Terminal Earth* message board says she has a pirated copy of it but that it's all shot from an angle and the time and date are burned into the bottom right-hand corner.

I can wait. I'm not that desperate.

I finish my homework before the lights come down— I can do my homework anywhere—and then the previews start.

Previews are like a little taste of candy. I give them

my full attention. I've already seen all the movies they're previewing because I see every single movie. I am always amazed at how much better the movie looks in its condensed form. It's like the potential of the film is better then the full-length reality.

Terminal Earth starts. I get that tingly excited feeling that I get every time I see it. I have seen it forty-two times already. I never get bored.

In honor of watching the movie today, I am wearing my best Egg outfit. Long white cloak, white pants, and white shirt. Hair freshly shaved to a buzzed perfection. Pale white skin. Colored eyebrows. Neutral lips. In the future there is no lipstick. Thank goodness for that. I'd be quite content with a world that doesn't force women to wear makeup to be beautiful. I'm sure it would destroy my mom though.

"How can you leave the house without your face on?" Mom says over and over again.

"My face is on," I have to say to her. "My plain, not beautiful, just normal, no-makeup-on face."

"Ugh, you make yourself boy proof on purpose," she always says.

And that's what I am. Boy proof.

I have never been asked out. No boy has ever even flirted with me. I am invisible to the opposite sex.

Egg is not boy proof though. She has a scar on her

face and she's got a bullet mark on her arm and a burn on her back and Uno still loves her.

The second time the film plays I examine every single aspect of Zach Cross as Uno. I love his crooked smile. The way he swaggers. His monosyllabic lines. The glint in his eye. The way he furrows his brow. He is so handsome.

I've seen every film that he's been in, but *Terminal Earth* is definitely the best.

I also examine the special effects, especially the makeup. I look for clues on how it was done. I look for flaws so I can learn. I am developing my effects eye.

The third time the film plays, I pay close attention again to the details of the story. There are going to be three films in all and I want to figure out any clues the filmmakers left in the first film. On the *Terminal Earth* message board there is a lot of speculation as to what's coming next.

I have my own ideas. I keep most of them to myself.

I stay until the last credit of the film rolls and then sit for a bit to digest it all after the lights come on. The usher comes in with his broom and garbage can. I wonder how much he gets paid to pick up the trash. I wonder if he's an aspiring actor, like the concession girl and the ticket-booth guy. Like everyone in Hollywood, except for me.

It's eleven o'clock, and when I get outside it's dark and a bit chilly. It might even rain by the time I get home. I walk briskly toward La Brea, past CBS Studio, past the Good Stuff natural supermarket, past the fancy restaurants and the Orthodox temples, then down La Brea to Third Street and over one short block to my house.

My Egg cloak doesn't cut the wind. I might have to winterize it. I think my dad has some fabric in his workshop that he used for some monster's hair that will work nicely as a lining. I'll check it out tomorrow.

When I get home, Mom is in the living room with a mud mask on her face. She's smoking a cigarette. A nasty habit. I cough to let her know it bothers me.

"You're supposed to smoke outside," I say.

"Well what am I supposed to do when I'm worried about where you are? I had to sit in here and watch the door. I'm sure I got two new lines on my forehead."

I put my keys on the hall table and head to the kitchen to see what leftovers I can eat. She follows me.

"It's not my fault you're not twenty-two anymore," I say.

She lets it slide.

Her mask is half dry. The dry parts are cracking as she speaks. The damp wet parts are like craters on a far-off planet. I laugh.

"Don't laugh, Victoria," she says. "What did I give you a cell phone for if you don't take it with you to school?"

"They cause brain cancer, Mom. Do you want me to get brain cancer?"

"Victoria. *Please*. Everything causes cancer."

"I would prefer if you call me Egg."

She knows this. I tell her all the time.

"Egg is not your real name."

I slam the fridge door shut. I have found a bag of baby carrots and some leftover mac and cheese.

"My meal will be fluorescent orange tonight," I say. "Very futuristic."

"It's eleven-thirty."

"Since when do I have a curfew?" I say.

"I hate you walking around the neighborhood at night."

"There are people around," I say. "And I'm not a baby."

"If you don't want to be treated like a baby, don't act like one."

The mask, now completely dry, is flaking off onto her pink silk bathrobe.

"Mom, you look like a lizard," I say.

She throws her hands up in the air and goes to the bathroom to wash the mask off.

I go to my room.

Mom always starts acting more motherly toward me when she hasn't had an acting job in a while. It's like all of a sudden she has too much time on her hands and nothing to do except get in my face about everything.

I wish she would just let me live with Dad. Dad is perfect, even if he is so focused on his work that you can't even say anything sometimes or he'll blow up at you.

Mom has to ruin that as well.

"He's just perfect because you only see him once a week," she says.

"You are just jealous because of how well Dad and I get along," I always say.

"You think I make your life hell? Living with your dad would make me seem like a kitten."

"Meow, meow," I hiss at her, clawing the air with my hands.

I can't wait to go to college and be on my own.

Middle of the Night.
Dreamland.
I'm dreaming about Zach Cross. He takes me to an L.A. Kings hockey game. They're playing the Toronto Maple Leafs. He's from Toronto. He rolls up his pro-

gram and whispers into my ear that he would like to make out with me but the paparazzi are watching. I think it is so great that he notices things like that. Later in the dream we find a utility closet at the Staples Center and make out. I am making out with Zach Cross. It is out of this world.

Tuesday. January 6. 7:30 A.M.
Zero Period.

That stinky new guy arrives late to AP Global History,
my favorite class. He sits in the front row right next to
Mr. Gerber's desk. Right in front of me.

"Nice of you to join us," Mr. Gerber says. "I expected you in this class yesterday."

"Hey, no problem, man," the new kid says, and I
notice he takes out a little sketchbook and places it on
the corner of his desk.

Mr. Gerber turns back to the board and writes *The
French Revolution* in his obnoxiously perfect cursive.
Mr. Gerber is wasting no time getting right back into
the semester. I like that. Then he turns back to us, his
mostly sleepy students, and he leans his hands on the
back of his chair and asks us, defeated, "Who can tell
me what they learned about the French Revolution in
their required winter-break reading?"

My hand shoots up in the air.

"Is there anyone else who's done the reading who wants to try before Miss Jurgen enlightens us once again?"

The class just shifts in their seats.

"It's called required reading, folks, because I *require* you to read it," Mr. Gerber says, exasperated. "This is an AP class. You actually have to do the work."

And then that new guy raises his hand.

"Mr. Max Carter, I'm pleased you've decided to jump right in. Do tell us all you know about the French Revolution."

I leave my hand in the air.

"Mr. Gerber, I always answer the question first," I say. "I always enlighten the class."

"Miss Jurgen, please," Mr. Gerber says.

This is my special class. This new guy doesn't know the protocol. So I lean forward and enlighten him.

"I always say my piece and then Mr. Gerber adds on to it," I say.

"Interesting," Max says. Then he flips open his little black sketchbook and jots something in it.

I hear everyone in the classroom start to snicker. I can imagine Rue behind me pressing her lips together and Nelly shaking her head down at her desk.

I don't care what they think.

"Max, why don't you share what you know about

the French Revolution and use your free time later to sketch," Mr. Gerber says.

"All right, Mr. Gerber. Basically when the monarch of an absolute monarchy is weak, it is easily brought down. The king, Louis the Sixteenth, was a very weak monarch. The nobles wanted power that had been taken away from them by the monarchy. The bourgeoisie resented the privileges of the nobles, and the bourgeoisie and the peasants criticized the tax system . . ."

Blah, blah, blah.

I stare at the back of Max Carter's greasy head. I want to look right into his brain and erase all he is saying.

He's showing off by adding little splashy details.

"Well, most of that isn't from the required reading; it's from the PBS documentary *The Revolution*," I say.

Max turns around and stares me down. He knows nothing about boundaries or personal space. He is looking too intensely at me. He is looking right down deep inside of me. I don't like it.

"I know," he says. "My dad made that documentary."

Oh, shit. Max *Carter*. His dad is Flint Carter, the documentary filmmaker.

I can hear the class breathing as one. They want to

see what's going to happen next. They're dying to see the fireworks.

"Well, Miss Jurgen," Mr. Gerber says, his mood brightening a little bit. "It looks like someone is finally going to give you a run for your money."

Then Mr. Gerber turns back to the board and pulls down a map of France and begins his lecture on the origins of the French Revolution.

Max is still turned around in his seat looking at me.

"Turn around, face front," I say to him.

"Yes, ma'am. Good to know who the autocrat is," he says, chuckling, and turns his eyes back to the front of the room.

"Is that an insult?" I ask.

"Yeah, you could definitely take it that way."

"And I'm a miss, not a ma'am," I say.

"Actually, you're neither. Those words apply to women of refinement," he says. Then he opens his sketchbook again and jots something down.

I jostle my desk into the back of his seat.

"Hey!" Max says. "Relax."

Rue, who is sitting behind me, reaches out and takes my arm.

"It's okay," she says to me. I shake her off.

"It is not okay," I say.

Mr. Gerber turns around. Clearly, I have committed some kind of classroom crime by slightly shoving my desk. I've never seen Mr. Gerber look so disappointed in someone before. I have been his best student all year.

"Miss Jurgen, I don't know what the problem is, but why don't you leave the room until you can calm down," Mr. Gerber says.

I shove my books into my army bag and walk out. Fuck that guy Max. He's a jerk. I notice he's the only one not freaked out by my behavior. He's not scared. He's actually chuckling as I leave the room. He's like a hyena, always laughing.

I head straight for the library. Straight for the history section. Straight for the French Revolution. I will know more about it than Max Carter and his stupid genius father.

Lunchtime.

Student Quad.

As a rule, I eat by myself, under a tree on the far side of the quad. But today I don't make it past the corner table, where the members of the Science Fiction and Fantasy Club sit every day, unseen.

16

"Egg! Egg!" Rue is shouting for my attention. She's so loud, I can't ignore her.

I'm caught.

Rue is patting the empty seat on the bench next to her with one hand and motioning for me to join them with the other.

Martin looks up at me with his moon-round face and smiles.

Martin is pear-shaped and doughy. His eyelashes are extremely long. He is sensitive and smart, but not as smart as I am. Rue is his girlfriend. She is thick-waisted but not really fat. She wears a scarf and a fedora hat all the time because she loves *Doctor Who,* but they don't go with her glasses and my mom would say that the browns wash out her pale skin. I think she should at least get rid of that old fedora or get over *Doctor Who;* I don't know which is more outdated.

Martin and Rue are so in love it makes me sick. They are in the kind of love you want to be in. They respect each other. They give each other space. They have individual personalities but they complement each other. I envy them.

I hate anybody in love.

I mean, how did two such geeks luck out so young? I think Rue is just as boy proof as me, and yet she has a boyfriend and I don't. Not that I would want Martin. Not that I care about any of the boys around here. I'm the only other girl in the club, but I wouldn't date any of these guys even if they were the last men on earth.

I want someone as cool as Uno.

"Question for you, Egg," Martin says.

"Shoot."

"We're having a debate about the most influential classic sci-fi film. I say it's *Star Wars*. Rue says it's *2001: A Space Odyssey*. And Hasan says *Blade Runner*. I'm sure you have an opinion."

Martin is so formal in his speech. He is a nerd and he has the unfortunate luck to sound all nasally like one, too. It makes me cringe.

"It's *The Day the Earth Stood Still*," I say.

"Oh. I hadn't thought of that one," Martin says.

"That's the one I meant. I change my answer to that one," Hasan says.

"Classic," I say. "Plenty of films borrow from it. Message of peace and all that."

"Egg, why don't you sit down and join us? Lunch is half over and you still haven't eaten," Rue says, patting the empty seat next to her again.

Mental note: Take different route over to tree at lunchtime.

"I gotta do homework," I say, making a hasty retreat.

Last Period.
AP English.

"What are you doing here?" I ask Max.

"I'm just sitting in my assigned seat," he says.

He's more interested in what *he's* doing than in me. So I bang around my books and the chair and the desk to show him how pissed off I am that he's sitting next to me again.

"Careful. You don't want a repeat of this morning," he says.

New tactic: Take matters into your own hands.

I push my way up to the front of the room and confront Mrs. Perez.

"I'd like for that new kid to be moved away from me," I say.

Mrs. Perez has her arms crossed and she's looking me over. She is sucking on a lozenge, which is making the hairy mole on her lip jump around. She always has a lozenge in her mouth, because she's always screaming and her throat always hurts.

"I place people in certain seats to maintain a certain

order in the classroom so that I won't have to yell as much."

"I had an incident with him this morning in Global History."

"Well, you won't have one here in my class or I'll fail you, even if you are one of my most gifted students."

Mrs. Perez is one tough cookie. That's what I like and hate about her.

"Well, he stinks," I say.

"Get over it."

The bell rings and she turns her back to me and picks up her stack of graded papers. I skulk back to my seat and sit down next to Max. I sniff loudly and make a face. He doesn't even smell today, but he continues to ignore me, which is highly annoying. He is busy with his pen and that little black book.

Now *I'm* interested in what he's doing.

"What are you doing?" I say.

"Drawing," Max says. "I study people. I draw them and take notes like an ethnographer."

I lean over and look at the black ink sketch he's made of my profile. There is a bubble under it that says, *Quick to anger, thinks she knows everything.*

It's a good rendition of me and he's made me look prettier than I really am, but I don't want to be in his book. I don't want to be collected.

I shoot my hand out to rip the page from its place. In anticipation of my move, he pulls the book away from me.

"Give it," I say.

"Nuh-uh," he says. "It's a social record."

"Look, I'm superstitious. You've drawn me. It's like you're stealing my soul or keeping my toenail clippings."

I throw him the evil eye.

"What are you trying to do?" Max says. "Get me with your superpowers?"

"You're an asshole," I say.

He laughs and continues sketching.

"Ars longa, vita brevis," Max says.

"What?"

"It's Latin," Max says. "It means 'Art is long, life is short.' This is art. This is forever."

He taps the drawings in his book adoringly.

"This," he says, drawing an imaginary circle around my face, "is not art. This does not have to be forever."

Mrs. Perez walks down the aisle toward us, passing back our environmental poems. She hands mine and Max's back. I hold it up for him to see: A+.

"Why don't you draw this?" I say.

"Why don't I draw *this* instead?" Max says, and holds up his poem: A++.

I grab for his paper and this time he lets me take it. I scan the poem for flaws, and my eyes fall upon these lines:

Silent is the ruined land.
Man is brutal
and the rain does not wash away
the pain
or rid the distant memory.
It makes it glisten.

I thought he was stupid. Now I know he's gifted, just like me.

4:00 P.M.
Sam Jurgen's Creature Shop.
An eyeless head is ogling me. I look over at the cemetery set from *Blue Hill Wyoming*. Skeletons are pushing up from the graves. On the walls are apes, monkeys, aliens, mummies . . . you name any creepy thing and it's there.

On a shelf to my left is the wall of blood. Jars and jars of fake blood and the ingredients for each kind.

My father, Sam Jurgen, master mask-maker, animatronic freak, monster and alien specialist, special-effects makeup wizard, is hunched over his worktable constructing the perfect eye.

I plop my bag down on a stool and remain quiet until he is finished. From years of experience, I know not to interrupt him while he's concentrating this hard.

Once, when I was about nine, I was bored and I wanted him to pay attention to me. He turned purple and shoved everything off the table onto the floor, then he yelled at me for getting in the way of the flow and ruining the lizard alien he was making. It's better to remain invisible until he turns his eyes on you. Once he does, he gives you all the careful attention you deserve. You just have to wait your turn.

"There," my dad says to me, holding up the eyeball.

Now it is okay to talk.

"Looks good," I say.

"No, really look at it," he says, and holds it under the work light. I lean forward and notice that the pupil dilates.

"Cool," I say.

He's like a little kid.

I can see pretty clearly why he and my mom didn't work out.

I try to imagine them falling in love while he applied

foam latex appliances and makeup to her on the episode of *The Nemesis* when she gets some weird skin radiation sickness and her whole face is peeling off.

Mom got kicked off the show when she got pregnant, and then Dad was doing his first big feature, a low-budget sci-fi film called *Star King,* which won him his first Academy Award. Soon after that, they split up.

She was mad about him applying lizard scales to all the naked models on the film, and he was mad that she wouldn't let him mix up the latex in the kitchen. I was probably screaming all the time, making them even more tired and annoyed.

"I can't believe that man-child won an Oscar before I did," Mom always says.

And I always remind her that she has never even once been considered for an Oscar, much less won one.

Freaks shouldn't breed, I think, looking at my dad while he works. *They end up having freaky kids like me.*

But as far as I can tell, as dads go, he's a good one. Every Tuesday I make my way over to his creature shop and we make stuff in silence. He even has the Victoria Tuesday clause put into his contracts, so when he's working in town we don't have to miss a date. It helps that he has a whole team of assistants.

"How's school?" he asks.

"Fine," I say.

"How's your mom?" he asks.

"Fine," I say.

"Do you have any boyfriends this week?" he asks.

"Nope," I say.

"Well, you're a catch," he says. "I wish I had known a girl who could design an alien exoskeleton."

I don't remind my dad that boys like that are total dorks.

8:00 P.M.

Living-Room Couch.

I'm reclining like a woman in a Matisse painting. I flick through the channels, jumping between the evening news on three different stations.

ABC: DEVASTATING FAULT DISCOVERED UNDER LOS ANGELES

CNN: DOCTORS PREDICT FLU PANDEMIC TO KILL MILLIONS

MSNBC: UNIVERSE INEXPLICABLY EXPANDING

"What's the news?" Mom says, shoving me over on the couch and pulling her salad out of the takeout bag. She pulls out my sandwich and hands it over.

"It's all doom and gloom."

"Oh, well. Did they announce the Screen Actors Guild nominees?"

"No."

I unwrap my sandwich and take a big bite.

"How was school today?" Mom asks, shifting full gear into mom mode.

"It sucked shit," I say.

"That is not the language a young lady uses," Mom informs me.

"I'm not a young lady," I say. "According to some new kid, I'm some kind of autocrat."

I grab my sandwich and get up so I can go eat alone in the privacy of my room, but she follows me down the hallway and she's talking, saying something that she probably thinks is important. I'm sure it's not, so I slam the door in her face as a response. Then I throw myself down on the bed and put my pillow over my head. Three, two, one . . .

The door opens and Mom barges into my room.

"Victoria—"

"It's *EGG*!!!" I scream. Maybe this time she will hear me.

"I'm not going to call you Egg," she says. "That's not the name I gave you."

"Well, Ursula's not your real name. Some agent gave you that name," I say.

"That's different. It's a professional name, not an item of food," Mom says.

I scream into my mattress.

"I'm meeting a director for drinks later," Mom says cheerfully.

"I don't care," I say.

Her weight makes the floor creak. She's put on some pounds since her glory days as the hot chick on the eighties TV show *The Nemesis*. She hasn't had a real role in years. She still looks like a model, though. My mom is gorgeous by anyone's standards. She is the total polar opposite of me.

She's standing there, waiting, hoping that I'll be impressed. She's hoping that I'll say what she always wants me to say to her before an audition or meeting. Even though I don't want to say it, I turn my head from under the pillow.

"Break a leg," I mumble.

I can see Mom smiling upside down. She's so happy I said it. She thinks it's going to bring her luck.

"I have a good feeling about this one. I'll be back later. Please be home when I get here."

I wave for her to go, go! GO! Move away! If I had a Helgerian laser like Egg does, I'd blow her out of my room.

I stay on my bed until I hear the jingle of her keys,

27

then the click of her high heels down the hallway. Then the door closes, and the lock snaps shut.

When I am sure she is gone, I log on to my computer. I set my play list on shuffle. Strains of Ella Fitzgerald fill the room. I surf over to the Zach Cross–*Terminal Earth* message board. No news today. He must still be in New Zealand filming the sequels. I check out some other sites of some other sci-fi films I'm tracking. I do a search on the guillotine. I read all about the Reign of Terror from 1793 to 1794. It freaks me out. It seems to me that the world has always sucked.

Amelissa13 instant messages me.

Amelissa13: hey eggtoria have you heard that Zach Cross broke his ankle?

Eggtoria: No shit.

Amelissa13: Just yesterday. It was in the papers here down under.

Eggtoria: that sucks.

Amelissa13: yeah. I thought I saw him at the movie theater in Christchurch, but it was just some old guy. But from far away, when I squinted, it totally looked like Zach Cross.

Eggtoria: I gotta go. Homework.

I shut my instant messenger off. I don't know why I even have it. Nobody in my real life chats online with

28

me. It's only those silly girls who like Zach Cross that do. I am different from them.

I'm not boy crazy. I have tried to explain it to them one million times.

I'm a cinephile.

Wednesday. January 7. 3:00 P.M.
Melrose Lion Meeting.

Here's something really weird. I love taking pictures for
the school paper.

"I've got contact sheets here, Nelly," I say, just to
hear myself say something out loud. My voice cracks a
bit from being unused all day long. Earlier today I took
a vow of silence.

"Drop them in the box, Egg. You know the rou-
tine," Nelly says. She smiles at me. She pushes her
glasses up on her pretty button nose.

My GPA is higher than hers.

Sometimes I almost think that I would like to be
Nelly Melendez's friend. She's the student editor of the
Melrose Lion. She's in all my AP classes. She's on the
tennis team. She has a brain.

She's chewing the eraser off a pencil and twisting
her really long brown hair with her skinny manicured
finger. And I bet even though she's looking up at me
that she doesn't know what I look like. I notice that she

never really looks in my eyes, as though I scare her. She treats me like I am an alien or a monster. She's afraid that she'll awaken the demon inside of me.

Nelly tries to be so nice—so welcoming, so understanding, so sweet, so everything a nice girl should be—that I try to convince myself that there is something deeply wrong with her. Like she's got some deep-rooted psycho issues.

But she's smart, and not a social retard like most of the people who talk to me, so I try with her. And I don't try anymore with anyone.

"I like your shirt," I say. "It's shiny."

Now she really looks up at me. I'm wearing my Egg cloak over jeans and a T-shirt.

"Yeah, um, I dig your cloak," she says. Only she says it like a question. Like I'm a joke. Like she's grabbing for straws to find something nice to say to me because she's *that* kind of nice girl. I convince myself of this because with me she always seems awkward. Forced. Fake. It upsets me, because there is nothing about me that she really digs.

She's finishing up the *Los Angeles Times* crossword puzzle that I already completed this morning while sipping on a latte and waiting for school to start. I can see that she can't get the answer for twelve down, "A Tolkien Tree."

I realize that she would never think to ask me for help. She probably just hopes I'll go away.

"It's 'Ent,'" I say.

"What?" Nelly says.

"The answer to twelve down."

"I would have gotten it eventually."

"Whatever," I say. "Just trying to be helpful."

I go and grab a seat for the meeting and wonder yet again why I try being friendly to people.

Mental note: Don't bother.

Ms. Dicostanzo comes in. I notice that she's put more blond in her hair and she has hip new chunky black glasses. She changes her look every four weeks. It corresponds to the exact same time all the new fashion magazines come out.

Max Carter is following her and they are deep in conversation. She pulls out a chair and Max sits next to her.

"Does he have to be everywhere?" I ask.

Nobody answers me.

"I'd like to introduce Max Carter, our new editorial cartoonist," Ms. Dicostanzo says.

"Do we need one?" I ask. "I mean, don't we have enough people on the paper?"

"There's always room for one more on the team!" Nelly says.

Ms. Dicostanzo nods in agreement.

Nelly leans forward in her chair trying to get a closer look at Max. Nelly likes everything new, and that includes boys.

"I think that there are already too many on the team," I say.

"Now, Egg, that's no way to treat a newcomer. Please welcome Max Carter to the *Melrose Lion*," Ms. Dicostanzo says.

Across the table, I see that Nelly's still checking Max out. I notice when she perks up, she pushes her chest out first and then rises in her seat. She fancies herself a kind of Lois Lane. I believe this might be an actual Nelly flaw. It makes me feel better. But Max Carter doesn't look like Clark Kent. I hardly think he's hiding a Superman outfit underneath his *Preacher* T-shirt.

"Wait, your name is Egg? Like in *Terminal Earth*?" Max asks.

I nod my head.

"Oh, now the cloak makes sense," Max says.

When I look up to meet his eyes, I notice that Max Carter has washed his hair.

"How do we know he can draw good?" Inez says.

Ms. Dicostanzo peers over her glasses at Inez.

"Please don't use street language here at the paper," she says.

"I was just being colloquial," Inez says.

Max holds up his sketchbook. It's a drawing of our mighty mascots, the Melrose Lions that guard the front of the building, dressed up to look like Charlie Chaplin and Buster Keaton. I have to admit that he's got talent.

"Oh," Nelly says. "That's cool."

"Do you even know who they are?" I say.

"You're not the only person who watches a lot of movies," Nelly says.

Nelly may be a cinephile, but it's only because she's starstruck. I bet she's never set foot in the Silent Movie Theater for one of their special screenings, even though it's practically across the street.

Then Nelly begins to hand out assignments.

"Okay, people. Egg, can you take pictures of the installation that went up two days ago at the empty lot down the street? The artists are being sued by the city, and I want coverage on the lawsuit. I'll write the story. Plus, I think it would be nice to document the art before the city tears it down."

I nod and tune out everything else she says until she tells us that we can go.

"Okay, that wraps it up. Good work, guys," Ms. Dicostanzo says.

I grab a new roll of film from the cabinet and head out of school and across the street.

3:56 P.M.

Corner of Melrose and Beverly.

"Hey. Wait up."

It's Max Carter. I don't want to share another single moment of my day with him. It is beginning to feel like he's living all over me. Enough already.

"I wait for no one," I say, and keep walking at my brisk pace. It's one of Egg's lines from the movie. It's one of my favorites. I quote her all the time.

The installation is beautiful. It is a model of the Statue of Liberty, made out of a broken gas pump.

I stand on the sidewalk looking through the chain-link fence.

"They tear everything down that's truly human," I say.

"Like Egg says," Max says.

"Yes, but it's true."

"I'd be interested in what *you* thought."

"Well, maybe art is only meant to last for just a moment, a wink in the span of the universe. Maybe it's a moment remembered and treasured. A private moment, one unshared."

"That's interesting," Max says.

"You think art is forever," I say. *"Ars longa, vita brevis."*

I'm sure I mangled the Latin.

35

"Well, you never know. Maybe I'm wrong," he says.

I take out my camera and start snapping. It's too bad I'm stuck out on the sidewalk. I'd like to get the details of the statue, but I don't have my zoom lens with me.

Mental note: A good photographer always has her camera. A great photographer always has the right lenses as well.

"You're too far away," Max says.

I keep my eye behind the lens and ignore him and make him invisible. *Snap. Snap. Snap.*

"Come on," he tugs at my cloak. "There's a way in over there."

I look up at him despite my desire to ignore him. He's heading toward the alleyway. I follow him. Lo and behold, there is a gap in the bottom part of the fence. He gets down on his hands and knees and crawls into the lot.

Once inside, he sticks his hand out from under the fence.

"Give me your camera so it doesn't get scratched."

I want to get inside. I look down the alley both ways. I'm a little afraid. But then again, Egg wouldn't be, so I shake off the fear. Egg would've scaled the walls or jumped the fence. She does what she wants. I do, too. I get down on my belly and slither into the lot.

Max hands me my camera and starts to walk toward the sculpture. He puts his backpack on the ground and takes out his sketchbook, sits cross-legged on the dusty ground, and starts to draw. He looks completely at peace, like a Buddha.

I move toward the sculpture. Lady Liberty's dress is made of watercolor-washed green magazine ads. They are cut in strips so that they flutter a little in the wind made by the heavy traffic coming off the street. Her feet are two rusted oilcans. Her body is the old gas pump. Her torch is the nozzle. A rod of iron holds her arm up high. Her crown of liberty is made of shredded tire. She makes me feel strong.

"Somebody thought this up," I say. "Somebody took the time to construct it and put it here."

"Yeah, ideas. They come and go, but this is *action*. This is like a whole sentence being spoken. It's like a quiet revolution," Max says.

That's exactly it.

"A point where something silent intersects with volume," I say.

I'm taken aback that someone can go there with me, since no one ever gets it when I speak. Usually there is so much explaining to do that I just keep my mouth shut, but it seems like Max could almost pluck the next thought from my head.

Suddenly it feels like I've been starving for meaningful talks with someone. It freaks me out. I turn my back to Max and get busy with more photograph taking.

"Come on," Max says after a while. "Let's go to Canter's and get a sandwich."

"Nah," I say. "Not hungry."

He shakes his head.

"You ought to try to be more social," he says, and then slips himself under the fence and heads down the street.

I stare at his retreating figure. I put the viewfinder of my camera up to my eye and take a picture of his back. I contemplate for one second meeting Max over at Canter's, but I change my mind and I go to Mäni's Bakery instead.

Thursday. January 15.
Between 6th and 7th Periods.
Hallway.

I notice that Max talks easily with people. He smiles easily. Engages easily.

I hear him make plans with everyone.

"We should totally do that!" he says about everything.

He's been here just over a week and already he knows every single person in the senior class. And they know him.

"Maybe I'll be valedictorian," I hear Max say to a group of people after class.

Maybe not, I think. *I will beat him. I will win.*

7th Period.
Trigonometry Quiz.
$3 \tan (x/2) + 3 = 0$

Twenty minutes have gone by and I'm still confused about question number one.

I actually consider cheating, but Ignacio is sitting next to me and I know for a fact that he won't do well on the test. He's an idiot. So I don't bother looking at his answer sheet.

I know I'm not supposed to waste time on just one question. My SAT prep class taught me that, so I move on to the next question. I plug in numbers. I pretend I know what I am doing.

The bell rings sooner than I think it should. I have barely finished filling out the exam.

"Whew! That was hard!" I say to no one in particular.

"Really?" Ignacio answers. "I thought that was really easy."

I had a sinking feeling at the beginning of the quiz that I was going to fail. Now, it morphs into a certainty.

After School. 3:02 P.M.
Dean of Students' Office.

Dr. Gellar, our dean of students, is annoyed with me because I am not getting to the point.

"Victoria, I have papers to grade."

"Okay, Max Carter has a higher GPA than me. But he transferred over from a school in England. So does that weigh in? I mean, he's been here just over a week. And they have a whole different system over there."

Dr. Gellar looks at me over her glasses.

"Max Carter hasn't even taken the SATs," I say. That's something that Dr. Gellar will understand for sure.

"Victoria, I don't know what you're getting at. If you're asking me if you're still in the running to be valedictorian, I suppose the answer is yes. You're a gifted student with an excellent academic record. You've had near-perfect attendance and are an exemplary student."

"You *suppose* the answer is yes?" I say.

"Victoria, these things aren't decided until all the grades are in, and there are many gifted seniors who are very close together in merit."

"But he just got here. It doesn't seem fair that someone can sneak in and steal away my place."

"Victoria, please stop wasting my time. I'm not going to guarantee anything until all the grades are in."

This answer will have to satisfy me. I push myself out of the metal chair, which unfortunately makes a horrible noise, and head out of Dr. Gellar's office. I am just about to close the door when I remember I should say thank you. No use in making her all mad at me. She might let my standing slip.

I poke my head back in.

"Dr. Gellar?" I say.

"What?" she snaps.

"Thank you," I say.

I close the door, pull an apple from my bag, and take a big bite out of it. It is delicious.

3:21 P.M.

Mr. Padilla's Physics Room.

Science Fiction and Fantasy Club Meeting.

"You're late, Egg," Martin says.

"So what?" I say. "I'm sure I didn't miss anything."

It is unfortunate that the Science Fiction and Fantasy Club is filled with geeks. But they are the only people that I can talk to ad nauseam about the kind of stuff I actually like. The truth is, socially, most of them are even worse off than me.

"Okay," says Hasan. "Who's in favor of taking a field trip to the Museum of Television and Radio and watching their screening of *Pilots of Science Fiction Television* on the thirty-first?"

We all raise our hands.

I agree to go only because I was planning on going anyway. No use in running into everyone there and making it be all weird. Might as well join the group.

"Don't forget that we have tickets to the midnight screening of *New Mars* tonight," Hasan says.

"*New Mars* is going to SUCK," I say.

"Egg, you say that about everything," Rue says.

"Not everything." Hasan comes to my defense, just to sound as though he has his own opinion. "And she's mostly right."

"I have high standards," I say. "I don't settle for flashy special effects and an overly dramatic soundtrack."

Martin winces. Those are his weaknesses. Martin only likes Hollywood science fiction. He's never read the books. He's never seen a foreign science fiction film or an indie science fiction film. No one here has. I like to see everything. So I always have the broader net to draw from.

"But I'm still coming to the screening," I say. "I'm always curious about a new space film. I hear they used a new technique on the animatronics for the Martians. I'm interested in seeing it in action."

We finish up some more club business and then the meeting is over.

Martin and Rue, the only people I can stand talking to, come up to me outside after the club meeting.

"We're going to the New Bev to see *Raiders of the Lost Ark* beforehand. Want to join us?"

"No can do," I say. "I've got my internship at the American Cinematheque."

I flick Rue's fedora with my fingers.

"Get rid of the hat, Rue."

"Get rid of the cloak, Egg."

She smiles at me. I want to smile back, but it might break me.

Egg is a woman who can't afford to get too close to anyone.

4:35 P.M.

American Cinematheque Offices.

"So I need you to label and stuff all these envelopes for the gala party," Wanda says.

There are about a million invitations.

"I'd like to go to the special screening of *A Dream for the Moon*," I say.

"I think Lark Austin has totally sold out," Wanda says. "This doesn't compare to her earlier, low-budget films. I can't believe she spent millions of dollars to make a film only to take all the color out of it in post-production. Why not just make it a black-and-white movie?"

"Saba Greer will be there with the director for a

Q & A," I say. "And the movie's not coming out in theaters for another two months."

Wanda likes obscure independent films. She programs all the cult films. She's a big purist. Unlike me she doesn't also like the big splashy Hollywood films.

"She plays Egg in *Terminal Earth*," I say.

"I know who she is, Egg. How could I not?" Wanda points at my cloak and smiles. She's not laughing at me, like other people do, and I like that most about her.

"How about I put you on duty for the special pre-film reception? You can help Eduardo set up the tables and then mingle at the party," she says.

"That would be great," I say, and then I stuff the envelopes with much more gusto.

In a little over a month, I will meet Egg herself!

Tuesday. January 20. 5:15 P.M.
Sam Jurgen's Creature Shop.

Making a life cast involves slathering someone's face with alginate. I know how to do it, but I don't have anyone to make a life cast of. So today, since Dad isn't so busy, he takes the time to make a new life cast of my face. I sit extremely still so I don't distort the mask. I am completely enclosed, ears plugged, senses shut off. The only thing I can hear inside my head is my own steady breathing and the strong sound of my heartbeat. Some people freak out during the process, but I like it.

When the alginate hardens, Dad pulls off the mother mold. I love seeing the inside of my own face.

I pour the plaster in to make a positive cast. I pull it out after about an hour and then I leave it to dry. Next week I'll have my own face to sculpt my creations on instead of a stock one that Dad has on the shelf.

I go over to the area where my positive from last week is waiting for me. I get the modeling clay and begin creating.

I like the way the clay softens in my fingers and how the monsters and aliens spring to life under my capable and sturdy hands.

I take the tools and make the pores in the face. I crease the line where a growl or a snarl is frozen in place. I determine the age of the character by the lines I press into the clay.

I am not doing this for anyone but myself.

I work and work and work silently next to Dad as he tinkers with an eyeball or an alien or ears that he needs to make for this project or that project. He is always tinkering.

After I spend two hours working and molding and pressing and poking the clay, Dad comes over to observe my work.

He turns the positive around. He circles it. He nods. He scrunches his face. He picks up a tool and adds something, an obvious wrinkle that I forgot.

"You're getting better, Egg," he says.

I make a two-piece mold over the entire head, then I open the mold and clean the clay out. I'm ready to make the foam latex. Soon, I will have a new mask for my collection.

"Document, document, document," Dad says.

I take out my camera and photograph the mask I finished painting last week.

"You have some great ideas for monsters," Dad says.

"My mind is a scary place," I say.

7:37 P.M.

King Kong Café.

I sit in the most out-of-the-way corner with my math book open. The numbers in the problems I am trying to solve morph into monsters. I abandon the math and begin drawing monster ideas in my notebook.

The light in the café is yellow, and I notice that everyone here is with someone else. They are with friends. I am the only one alone. I throw my Egg cloak over the empty chair at my table so it looks like someone is coming right back to sit with me. So that the chair looks occupied.

It's 7:37 P.M., by the big antique clock on the wall. The café starts to fill up.

A girl comes over to me. She is wearing nerdy cat eyeglasses with rhinestones in them. One of the rhinestones is missing. It looks like a gap tooth. She doesn't seem to mind the moth holes in her green sweater, or her greasy, faded pink hair, or the obvious paint crusted onto her jeans. I notice she wears her piercings with much more ease than I do.

Bitch, I think.

"I noticed you sketching," she says.

"I'm doing my homework."

"We're doing a *bande dessinée en directe* here tonight. I could give you a board to draw on."

"I don't have any money."

"You don't need money. I give you a board and then you draw on it and then give your drawing to someone else to ink and then we collect them and make a mini-comic out of it. See?"

She slips me a mini-comic.

"This is from the last event," she says.

"I'm not really a joiner," I say.

Unfazed, she moves on to bother the people at the next table. They eagerly take a board from her.

I put my notebook down and look around at the other people in the room. I look at the person at the next table. He's drawing stupid stick figures. I draw way better than that.

Maybe I *could* draw something. I get up to find pinky nerdy girl with the blank boards.

"Oh, great!" she says as she hands me my board.

I can always leave, I say to myself. *I don't have to have anyone ink my pencil picture.* I start to walk back to my table and run right into Max Carter. My blank board falls to the ground. Max picks it up.

It takes me a long time to find a place that I can call

my own. Somewhere I won't run into anyone I know. Somewhere I can be alone. And yet here is Max, invading my territory, *again*.

"Hey. Wow. I didn't know you did stuff like this," he says.

"I don't," I say.

He laughs. "Yeah, obviously not."

"No, really, it's an accident that I'm here. I didn't know they were doing this tonight."

"Do you have an inker yet?"

"No. I'm probably not going to even do it."

"Where are you sitting? Let me get a board and we'll ink each other's drawings."

He leaves me there to go off and find his own board. I shouldn't let a stupid blank board drive me into a fit of not doing anything. I go back to my seat. I feel fluttery, like I am on a tightrope. I am exposed in the air. Naked. Out of my element. Feet not on the ground. The fluttery feeling turns into nervousness. Which then turns into anger. Which then turns into action.

I attack my blank board. I start with wide lines and circles and begin to draw my newest alien creations, the ones I am keen on making into masks.

Max moves my cloak from the back of the other chair and begins to draw. We don't even talk once, even though the café is buzzing with conversation. The silence stretches out between us, and that suits me just fine.

After a bit Max hands me his board.

I scan it. It's a sketch of an apartment building with eight windows. Each window reveals a scene about the loneliness of the person inside. Growing up the side of the building is a vine of flowers.

I don't say anything about the drawing, but it moves me.

"It's an idea I have for a story in the graphic novel I'm working on."

I nod.

He takes a marker out and starts on the board with my multiple monster alien faces on it.

"I love the way you draw with such detail," he says. "Where do you get your ideas for these?"

"My dad's workshop, I guess," I say.

I decide to ink his drawing in grays and blacks, but make the flowers a hopeful dusty pink.

"I'm glad I found this café," he says. "It reminds me of a place where I used to hang out in London. They were always doing cool shit like this there."

"Uh-huh." I say.

I don't know how to make small talk. But Max does.

"It's essential, don't you think, to find a place that you can call your own?"

"Yeah," I say. "I really don't like to run into people I know."

"I know, me neither." Max says. "I like to be alone sometimes. Especially when I'm drawing. Especially when I'm doing stuff like this."

Suddenly I find it strange. Max and I are sitting together and yet somehow I feel just as clear as when I'm alone.

"I think clearer, study better, when I'm alone in a café," I say.

"Me too!" Max says. "Even though there is so much going on around me, I feel like I'm in my own world."

"In the flow," I say.

He nods as he picks up another marker color to add to one of my monsters.

"Some people go to cafés just to see and be seen," Max says. "I hate that they don't get it."

"No one ever sees me," I say.

"Yeah, right." He laughs. "You're invisible, Egg."

But that's how I feel. I'm the Invisible Girl.

Wednesday. January 21. Lunchtime.
Student Quad.

Max approaches me in the quad, hand extended, offering me a bottle of sparkling water. I take the bottle reluctantly.

"Hey, can I sit here?"

"I'm not in the mood for small talk," I say. "I'm studying."

But my math book is on the bench next to me and I'm actually reading a novel.

"Really?" Max says.

"What does it look like?"

"It looks like you could use some company," he says. "Why didn't you tell me last night that your father is *the* Sam Jurgen? No wonder those alien faces you drew are so kick-ass."

"It didn't come up," I say.

"God. I loved his work in *Star King*," Max says. He sits down next to me, uninvited, and opens up his bottle of water. His head tilts back as he swallows most of it in one gulp. "When they cut that lizard alien out of its mother's stomach and it has the mark of the king. Wow!"

"I'm kind of reading."

"Yeah, I remember when I went through my Dick stage," he says.

"What did you call me?" I ask.

He points to the novel I'm reading. It's by Philip K. Dick. I feel like an idiot.

"So let me get this straight. You're telling me that you *prefer* to eat lunch alone every day?" Max says.

"Yes," I say.

"Okay. I respect that," he says, tossing his empty bottle into the recycling bin. "You know, you're a real puzzle."

"I'm not something to be solved," I say.

"*De gustibus non est disputandum,*" Max says, and walks off.

Middle of the Night.
Dreamland.
Zach Cross is unhooking my bra and kissing the nape of my neck.

"What do you think about love, Egg?"

Just like in the movie, we look up at the sky. There are needleships hovering in place above us.

"I think it's all about smell," I say.

He breathes in my scent and whispers in my ear, "I think you smell like hope."

He kisses me, and unlike in the movie, the needleships fall to the ground, setting off an apocalyptic fireball.

"The world is a dying place," I say.

"I expect it to end hourly," Zach says. Then he flames out. Dead.

I wake up. It's 2:37 A.M. and I'm not sleepy anymore. I pick up my Dick book, *Do Androids Dream of Electric Sheep?* and begin reading. It must be hours later that I finally fall back asleep.

Thursday. January 29. 7:44 A.M.
Bed.

"Victoria." Mom knocks on my door. "You're late for
school."

Shit.

I scramble out of bed and throw some pants on. I
don't bother changing my shirt—it's too cold to take it
off. I rub some jasmine oil on my skin, brush my teeth,
and fly out the door.

Global History is half over.

"Do you have an excuse?" Mr. Gerber asks.

"I overslept."

"Invest in an alarm clock, Miss Jurgen." He turns
back to the chalkboard and begins arranging all the
French Republics onto a timeline.

I open my notebook and start to take notes. The
pages are blurred because I am crying. I have never been
late to Global History before. It's my favorite class and
Mr. Gerber is my favorite teacher. It's the only thing
worth coming to school for.

"You smell good today," Max Carter turns around and whispers.

I don't answer him.

"Are you crying?" he asks.

"I don't cry."

A tear falls onto my loose-leaf paper, making me a liar and smudging the words *Third Republic*. Max Carter's hand slips a little package of Kleenex through my arms and onto my notebook. The Kleenex is from Japan. It is pink and it has little goofy characters on it. I take a piece out and wipe my eyes. It feels like everyone is looking at me.

Except Max Carter. He's leaving me alone, just like I asked him to.

7th Period.

Math Class.

During the trigonometry quiz, instead of solving any of the problems, I notice that the whole world is made up of angles and arcs. If I squint just the right way, I can make anything look like an angle.

I can see me in relation to the rest of the world. I am x. The pen in my hand, my elbow, and the distance to my empty brain is a math problem. I can vary the arc. The pen is x.

The bird in the air, outside the window, flying to the tree is unconsciously measuring the arcs and angles. I can see the math all around me.

But when it comes to putting it down on paper, I draw a blank.

One thing I can answer for sure. I'm going to fail another quiz.

Saturday. January 31. 1:14 P.M.
Field Trip: Museum of Television and Radio.

I am in the gift shop, next to Hasan, who is nearly pee-ing his pants over all the DVDs of TV shows they have. He's bought nearly everything in the store.

"If I bought the first season of *The Nemesis* on DVD, could you get your mom to sign it for me?" Hasan asks.

"No," I say.

"Oh, come on," Hasan begs. He is so geeky it's embarrassing.

"You'll sell it on eBay or something," I say.

"No, he would only do that if he bought two copies," Martin chimes in.

"I'm so in love with your mom, Egg. If I was older or she was younger, I would ask her out on a date," Hasan says.

"That's pathetic," I say.

"I can't see any of your mother in your face," Hasan says. "You must look like your dad."

"Ugh," I say, and roll my eyes at the pins and mugs under the glass counter.

"Is there really a need for this much *Nemesis* stuff?" I say.

In the screening series, they showed the *Nemesis* pilot. My mom, prancing around in a skintight catsuit before she got knocked up with me.

It's embarrassing.

It's unfair.

She was hot and I am not. Under my layers of clothing, there is not such a toned skinny body as hers was. I have curves. I have boobs.

"I would have loved to have had your boobs," Mom always says. "Why do you always hide your body? You should emphasize your assets. You make yourself ugly on purpose."

"Boy proof," I remind her.

"The museum is going to have a *Nemesis* marathon for its twentieth anniversary," the gift-shop guy says. "There is going to be a reception and everything. The whole original cast is going to be here."

"I haven't heard about that," I say. "I would know."

"Well, it's true. That's why I'm so stocked on *Nemesis* stuff right now."

"Cool," Hasan says. "Can we come with you to the reception, Egg?"

"No," I say.

I leave the gift shop and slam the door on my way outside to be by myself.

I wish I smoked cigarettes or had a flask or did something self-destructive to get rid of this burning black feeling inside of me. Instead I resort to biting my nails. If the world were going to end, like in *Terminal Earth*, I wish it would do it right now on top of me.

"What ho!" Rue says, offering me half of her tofu sandwich.

I shift away from her.

"You wouldn't understand," I say.

"Try me," she says. She's being sincere. She's being genuinely nice. She probably tells people that she's my friend, but I can't get past the sprouts stuck in her teeth.

"No way."

Rue's face sinks, like I've punched her. And, in a way, I have. She'll bounce back, though. I've noticed that Rue has somehow acquired those kinds of skills.

8:20 P.M.
Kitchen.
"Ten times, I must have mentioned the invitation to you. I even put it on the fridge," Mom says.

"No, it's not true!" I say.

"I give up," Mom says, and leaves the house for her dinner date.

I walk over to the fridge and there it is, an invitation to the twentieth anniversary of *The Nemesis* TV show at the Museum of Television and Radio.

I hate when Mom is right.

Mental note: When you pick your battle, make sure it's one you can win.

Sunday. February 1. 11:00 P.M.
Living-Room Couch.

MSNBC: DEFORESTATION OF WILDERNESS RESERVE

ABC: BIRDS SLICKED WITH OIL FROM A TANKER SPILL

CNN: COLOR CODE CHANGED: TERRORIST ATTACK IMMINENT

"How's the news?" Mom asks, bringing me my dinner, freshly ordered in from the coffee shop down the street.

"Not good," I say, cracking open my meal in a box.

Mom takes the zapper and channel-surfs to *E! True Hollywood Story,* which doesn't make the whole wide world look or sound any better.

I head down the hallway to my room. I'll do my English homework first. It's easier. I'll attack the trig before bed, so that the answers to the problems seep into my sleep.

English homework assignment: What is your personal philosophy of life?

I take pen to paper.

They are destroying everything anyway, so what's the point?

Later.

Bed.

I try to fall asleep, but I am filled with the thought that I am powerless. I open my mouth but I have no voice. I cannot scream. The cars on the street suddenly sound like missiles falling, like in *Terminal Earth*.

I lie there and I listen, afraid, heart beating fast, so loud in my ears I want to yell, Shut up, shut up, SHUT UP!

What if this is it? What if I have to live through the end of the world, like they do in the movies? To me, this *is* the end of the world. To me, this is real. I try to get out of the house, away from the bombs.

I wake up on the living-room floor.

My knee is skinned and bleeding. I start to laugh at myself for being so stupid as to believe a dream was real. Even worse, I'm still clutching my trigonometry textbook.

"What's going on out there?" Mom asks. She's run out of her bedroom, scared by the noise I am making. She thinks it is an earthquake.

"Nothing," I lie. "I just fell."

"Well, what are you doing up at this time of night?"

"I was going to make myself some Sleepytime tea."

"Oh, no, Victoria, I don't want the kettle screaming at this hour. I have to get some beauty sleep. I have a seven A.M. call tomorrow."

My mom finally has a new job. She is playing Mrs. Claus in a Movie of the Week. This means freedom from her always trying to bond with me and asking questions. At least for the next little while.

"Okay," I say. I will microwave the water. She will never know. I need to sleep tonight. Tomorrow there is another quiz in trigonometry and I have to pass. I am slipping. I feel myself slipping.

I turn the computer on and log on to the *Terminal Earth* site.

Geranium7: Hey Eggtoria. Are you going to the A Dream for the Moon *screening at the Cinematheque? Saba Greer is going to be there. I am going to take the train up.*

Eggtoria: yep.

Geranium7: We are all going to go and try to meet Saba Greer. We have decided to all wear a white rose on our cloaks, so that we'll know each other.

Eggtoria: Got it. White rose.

Geranium7: Ok see you there. Can't wait to finally meet you.

Mental note: Do not wear anything Egg-like at the A Dream for the Moon *reception.*

Anyway, there is no chance in hell that I would ever wear a flower on my cloak. I am curious, though, to see what everyone else looks like. I wonder if they're as boy proof as I am. I worry that I am really the most awful girl ever.

Knock, knock. My instant messenger says, *Do you want to accept a message from Catburglar?*

Catburglar. Who is that? I don't know that name. I am intrigued. I accept.

Catburglar: Non est ad astra mollis e terris via.
Eggtoria: What? Who is this?
Catburglar: That's my philosophy. It's a quote from the past. "There is no easy way from the earth to the stars." I got your info off the Lion *contact sheet. I thought I was the only one who couldn't sleep.*

Max Carter.

It blinks at me. Begging for a reply.

His philosophy is so right. So multilayered. I wish that I had thought of it. It even looks good written in Latin. I would like to engage in a discourse about what exactly "earth" and "stars" mean. I want to talk about how even if there is no *easy* way to the stars, there still *is* a way. I bet he would have something clever to say about it. But I wonder if my words would look as pretty as his, written and blinking on the computer screen.

I log off. Suddenly I don't feel like chatting.

Monday. February 2. 7:10 A.M.
Melrose Prep Front Entrance.

I grab a PowerBar and head to school.

"I tried IM'ing you last night. Why'd you log off?"
Max walks up to me.

He hands me a clementine section. I accept it; the
juice squirts in my mouth and tastes good.

"I didn't feel like chatting. I was studying."

"What did you do this weekend?" Max asks.

The sun is making his eyes glitter. They are blue
with flecks of yellow. I put up my defense field.

"The Science Fiction and Fantasy Club went to the
Museum of Television and Radio."

I am afraid that Max is going to make fun of me. I
am prepared for it.

"Go ahead, make your lame geek jokes," I say.

"Why? I love sci-fi," Max says. He lifts up the
sleeve of his T-shirt and shows me his ankh tattoo.

I'm surprised at how sculpted his arm muscle is. I
didn't have him pegged as a person who lifts weights.

His skin is incredibly white. I reach out and touch the ink. The tattoo looks as though it should feel raised, but it's not—it's smooth.

I feel a shock. He doesn't seem fazed at all. He goes on talking.

"It's from *The Sandman* and also from *Logan's Run*."

"I know, death, sanctuary. Whatever. Big deal, you like sci-fi," I say.

"One thing that I really love about sci-fi and fantasy is how they talk about taboo issues and open up a conversation about them," Max says. "That's how I started to become politically aware."

I think about that for a moment. I knew it already but hadn't really articulated it before.

"Like *Terminal Earth* talks about environmental apocalypse and drug resistance," I say.

"And fear of the other," he adds. "So, see, I love it. I love sci-fi. I just love real life, too."

Max points at the nuclear radiation symbol on my T-shirt. His finger brushes the side of my breast, though he doesn't seem to notice. Instead, he pulls his sketchbook out of his backpack as we are walking to Global History.

"I wanted to show you this," he says, and opens the book to a picture of the Gas Pump Lady Liberty. It's his editorial cartoon for the *Melrose Lion*. It is the Gas

Pump Lady Liberty sculpture draped with furs and boas and diamonds. In the corner of the drawing are the backs of the paparazzi who are taking pictures of her. The caption says "Real Art for the Angelino."

"This is great, Max," I say, looking at him with my real eyes, to let him know I mean it.

I gently take the book from his hands and run my fingers over the thick paper, feeling the way the ink bumps and scratches. I can tell that the pressure Max uses on the pen is as intense as he is.

"I wanted to show you first." He nods at me like a co-conspirator. Like we're friends.

8:34 P.M.

Home.

"Victoria, do you want to make some money for yourself?"

"Money is power in this corrupt world," I say. "What do I have to do?"

"You would be an Awkwardly Tall Elf," Mom says. "There are a lot of tall elves at the North Pole, and Santa is beginning to worry. It's only for one Saturday."

I don't want to be an Awkwardly Tall Elf, but I do want to have my own money. I want freedom. I want independence.

"Are there prosthetics for the elves?" I ask.

"Yes, I think so. Why do you ask?" Mom says.

I look at her, dumbfounded.

"Two reasons, Mom." I have to spell everything out for her. "One, I want so much makeup on that no one could possibly ever recognize me. And two, I like special-effects makeup. Try to keep up with the details of my life, okay?"

"We really aren't cut from the same cloth, are we?" Mom says.

"No, we aren't," I say. "I'm just like Dad."

Mom presses her lips into a line and grinds her teeth. I watch her count to ten and exhale. I know exactly which buttons to push to drive her crazy.

Middle of the Night.
Dreamland.

"Twice they fell between the rocks of Gron Golder. And we would not make the same mistake again," I say.

Zach Cross sticks his finger in my mouth and lowers himself to my lips in a kiss.

"They're coming," he says. He is Uno now. He is wearing his tight black T-shirt and patent-leather pants. His hair is gelled back. His sunglasses are on. I hear the enemy scuttling toward the door.

"No!"

The guns are out. The shooting begins. Uno crumbles to the floor, and when I turn the body over, I discover that it's Max that's lying there dead.

I wake up in a sweat. I go to the bathroom and splash some water on my face. I know why I am having these nightmares. I go back to my room and pull this week's trigonometry quiz out from underneath my mattress: 52%, it says. Next to it is a red frowny face.

It is the worst grade I have ever gotten in my life.

I cannot fail. Can. Not. Fail.

I open up my trig textbook and begin to study. There is a whole new chapter to learn. I've read it twice, but I still feel weak about it. Astronauts use this to calculate stuff. Egg knows these equations so she can pilot her planes. I should know it, too.

The worry is eating me alive.

Tuesday. February 10. 10:04 A.M.
Gym Class.

I always wait until the second bell rings before I begin slowly taking off my street clothes and putting on my gym clothes. I don't want anyone to see my body, but I have to get out onto the gym floor before the late bell rings. It's a fine balance of time. And I have to make it work. Six late marks equal failure.

I slide my eyes over to the girls who know how to stand nonchalantly in underwear, just chatting. The group includes Nelly and Inez. Nelly's leg is up on the bench between the lockers and she is rubbing glitter lotion onto her calves.

How did girls like that become so comfortable with their bodies? How did I miss out on that lesson?

I am uncomfortable in this body.

I cannot wear a cute tank top with confidence.

I listen like a fly on the wall. It doesn't matter to them that I'm there. Because I'm the Invisible Girl.

"Well, I think Max Carter is cute," Nelly says. "There's just something about him."

"Yeah, but he's always got his nose in that little sketchbook. It's kind of creepy," Inez says while fixing the braids in her hair.

"It's not creepy. It's mysterious. He's totally driven," Nelly says. "He's really smart and cultured. He's so not a boy."

I suck my lips in and mock her to myself.

"Maybe you should ask him out," another girl says.

"Yeah, maybe I should. I love talking to him. He's so deep."

The lockers slam shut and the voices echo down the hallway to the door to the gym until it's just me and the tick of the large caged clock.

I smart a little. A pinprick. I'm used to envy, but this pain is different.

Max Carter has deep conversations with someone other than me.

4:13 P.M.

Sam Jurgen's Creature Shop.

There is something about my face that looks all wrong. I can't put my finger on it.

I circle the positive of my own head and examine it carefully, making notes.

I could extend my brow. Bubble it out. Turn it into a classic-looking extraterrestrial.

I could make my nose gill-like and turn it into an aquatic creature.

I could thin out my lips. I could remove my own mouth. I could round out the chin.

Dad looks up from adding tiny pearls next to the eyes that cover the shell of a sea monster. *Kilnoa of the Deep* is the name of the film he is currently working on.

"See how the actor will fit in here?" He points to a small compartment in the shell.

I move off my bench and circle the shell to the back where wires and grips make up the servomechanism that will move the hundreds of tiny eyes on the shell.

"How long will it take the actor to get made up?" I ask.

"About six hours. It will be a lot like torture," Dad says. "But it's going to look fantastic."

My dad is beaming. He can make something from someone's most outrageous imagination turn real.

"The idea is that pollution in the ocean is irritating the giant mutant shells, and they're not just producing harmless pearls anymore," he says.

The wheels in my mind start to spin.

"What's up?" he asks.

"Nothing," I say.

I take some of the clay and slap it on the positive. I will turn myself into a birdlike creature, slicked with oil. I pull an old newspaper out of the garbage can, one with the pictures of the thousands of birds caught in an oil spill. I rip out the biggest picture and bring it back to the table to use as a guide.

Dad glances at the picture.

"What a tragedy," he says. He notices the beak I have begun to extend on the cast. "You going to use the picture as a guideline?"

"Yes," I say. "I'm going to make a statement."

Wednesday. February 11. Lunchtime.
Student Quad.

I watch from my usual spot at lunch instead of concentrating on my Global History textbook. Nelly is talking to Max Carter. She is sticking out her breasts. She's pushing her cute glasses up on her nose. She's presenting him the nape of her neck. She wants him to bite it.

I dissect Nelly. She's pretty, but not *that* pretty. She's normal. She's nice. She's friendly.

Now that Max sits with Nelly, he never comes and tries to sit with me. In this one small moment of scrutinizing Nelly, I have to admit that Max has good taste in preferring to sit with her over me.

Maybe I'd like to be her. Maybe if I tried, I *could* be her. Then again, maybe not.

Even history's steady march can't keep my attention today. I begin to doodle in the margin of my notes while nibbling at my sandwich.

Finally I give up on eating. I'm not hungry. I fold the plastic wrap back around my sandwich. Maybe I'll be hungry later. Max finishes his conversation with Nelly and walks away. He walks toward me. I move over on the bench to make more room for him.

What do I think I'm doing?

But Max doesn't even look up as he passes me by. He leaves me alone just like I want. Just like I told him every day when he tried to sit with me.

He walks by without stopping to show me that he respects my space. But I feel disappointed, like maybe for once I want something different to happen. Maybe for once I do want the company.

3:12 P.M.

Melrose Lion Meeting

Ms. Dicostanzo sweeps into the *Melrose Lion* meeting. Everybody looks up from the work they're doing on the new issue. She's holding up the school paper that came out earlier today. She's beaming.

"This is the best issue for which I have ever had the privilege to be faculty editor. Give yourselves a round of applause."

She starts clapping, and her French-tipped nails click and her spangly bracelets bang together. She is a noisy person.

Everyone claps along, because, I've noticed, people like to appreciate themselves.

I'm the only one not clapping.

"Egg, your photo-essay is fantastic. Nelly, your story is inspired. And Max"—she beams at Max, who looks at his folded hands—"you are *sublime.*"

"Yeah, it's such a great cartoon, Max," Nelly says, her eyes all glittery.

"I'm just warming up," Max says. He's blushing. Nelly makes him blush.

What is it that makes those two people attracted to each other? Certainly they don't have much in common. They could only have limited conversations, I'm sure of it. Even if Nelly thinks they are deep.

"I'm so proud that I'm entering this trio into the statewide student journalism competition. I think we really stand a chance," Ms. Dicostanzo says.

Ms. Dicostanzo likes doing stuff like that. It makes her look good.

"Okay. Down to business," Nelly says, chest out, pencil in corner of mouth, which makes her look serious. "Anybody got any leads on any cool stories?"

I raise my hand.

"Egg, that's nice of you to participate," Nelly says.

I grimace. She just has to point out that I am antisocial.

"There's a comic book, sci-fi, and horror convention

in Pasadena. There's going to be an exhibit of masks and animatronics from the great masters from movies like *Dracula* to *Terminal Earth*," I say.

Some people snicker.

Nelly, trying to be the best student editor she can be, pretends to mull it over a minute.

"The exhibit is going to end up at the Smithsonian. It's an important exhibit," I add.

"That's more entertainment-oriented, and I think the *Lion* should be a serious paper," she says.

"I agree," Inez chimes in. "We get enough entertainment news every day with all of Hollywood surrounding us."

"It's Hollywood *history*," I say. Why don't they get it?

"Good suggestion, Egg. I'm glad that you're beginning to participate. I'm sure you could find some e-zine that would love for you to cover it for them," Ms. Dicostanzo says.

"Good point," Nelly says. "Anyone else?"

Max raises his hand.

"I think we should cover the Buns Not Guns show taking place downtown this Sunday," he says.

"Buns Not Guns?" says Inez. "What kind of show is that?"

"It's an organization that sends food to needy

communities around the world, instead of weapons," explains Max.

"Oh," says Inez. "That's cool."

I'm looking out the window, listening, but from a distance. Buns Not Guns has an interesting ring to it. I look over at Max and he is standing there matter-of-factly. His face is serious and it's obviously something important to him. There is clarity in his eyes. A focus. His thinking it's important piques my interest. It compels me to sit up and take notice. It makes me want to go and check it out.

"Ooooh. That sounds so alternative," Nelly says. "I'll go with you and review it."

I catch Max as he slides Nelly a smile.

"What time should I pick you up?" he asks.

"I have to go to the bathroom," I say, and I grab my army bag and leave the meeting. I am sweating. I feel feverish. The cool air outside makes me feel better. I walk out of the building, off of school grounds, and head for Golden Apple Comics. Martin is working today. I will buy some comic books, and I will feel better.

4:36 P.M.

Golden Apple Comics.

"Hey, Egg, I got some new titles put aside for you," Martin says. "*Bota Life, Ratgirl, The Justice Clan . . .*"

"Oh, yeah. Cool." I am distracted.

If I were in a comic book, I would be the superhero, the one who was laughed at in school but was truly a genius. The Invisible Girl in my real life, Extraordinary Girl in disguise.

"I think you're really going to like this new post-apocalyptic series called *BenBoy,*" Martin says. "It's like science fact and future environmental crisis distopia with a twist of coming plague."

"Uh-huh," I say.

If I were a survivor at the end of the world, I would load my vehicle up with food and water and single-handedly save humanity. I would seem so gruff that no one would know about my loving, caring heart. Its absence, I am convinced, would be greater proof that it was there.

I walk around the store and look at the action figures and new comics.

"Guess what I heard today on the Net?" Martin says, coming up behind me.

"What?"

"The *Terminal Earth* DVD is coming out in April."

I stop dead in my tracks and close my eyes. At last, one piece of good news. My shitty day has been saved.

"But they announced the release date for the summer," I say.

"That's going to be the special edition. This first one is just going to be the movie, with no extras on it."

"That's great news," I say. "That's fucking kick-ass."

"Hey, you know who seems pretty cool?" Martin says.

"No, who?" I say.

"That new kid Max," Martin says.

I feel like I'm going to throw up.

"What?" Martin says.

"I don't know. He kind of annoys me," I say.

"I asked him if he wanted to join the Science Fiction and Fantasy Club, but he said no," Martin says.

"Why would you ask *him* to join?" I say.

"The guy had me write a list of thirty-two comics to track and collect for him. Stuff from everywhere. He's got great taste," Martin says. "And he bought a whole bunch of action figures. Obscure stuff."

"Whatever. Catch you later," I say, forking over my cash for the comics. I would love to get a peek at that list, though. I'm sure his taste in comics lies close to my own. How could Nelly ever appreciate the fine passion of comic-book collecting?

"Oh, and hey," Martin says.

"What?"

"I really liked your photo-essay in the *Lion* today."

"Thanks," I say, and smile. It feels more like a grimace. Smiles don't set well on my face.

I pull my cloak together and walk home.

7:32 P.M.
Home.

There are a bunch of projects I need to finish. I pull out the sewing machine and unbag the fabric I got from Dad's workshop and begin working on winterizing my Egg cloak.

I don't need a pattern. I eyeball the fabric and rip and tear and edge and age the cloak with ease.

"I can't work when you're hovering." I don't look up, but I know that my mom is standing right behind me.

"Sorry," Mom says, and undoes herself from standing still. The energy in the room all of a sudden moves more freely. Mom comes up right next to me. She has too much perfume on. She must have a date.

My fingers fly on the machine; my foot pumps.

"You really are very crafty," Mom says.

"Thanks," I say.

"You could be a fashion designer. That might be a good career for you. Paris Fashion Week. Milan. Rome. I could sit in the front row. 'Victoria Jurgen, Ursula Denton's daughter, showed her new line this week.'"

Even my mom's fantasies about me star her.

"Mom," I say.

"What?"

"Let me make something perfectly clear so that there is no possibility for a misunderstanding."

"Okay."

"I'm not ever, never, ever, not at all ever, going to become a FASHION DESIGNER!"

"But you have a gift," Mom says.

I hold up my finished cloak and put it on. It fits perfectly.

Mom follows me into the hallway.

"Where are you going?" she asks.

"Out."

"No, Victoria. It's a school night."

I stick my fingers in my ears to show her that I'm not listening. I walk out the door and into the dark, dark night.

84

Home.

"Hello?" I yell into the apartment.

"Well, at least I don't have to spend any more time worrying this evening. Thank you very much," Mom says.

She's in the living room with her feet up, smoking a cigarette and drinking a glass of red wine.

I cough. I grasp my throat. I throw my book bag on the living-room floor. I fall to the ground and twitch.

Mom applauds.

"Bravo, Victoria," she says. "I don't know why I'm the actress in the family when clearly you have all the talent."

I prop myself up on my elbows, and Mom does me the favor of stubbing out her cigarette.

"Okay. Now that I'm done being angry with you, I've got a surprise for you," Mom says.

"Really?" I say. "I kind of doubt it."

"No, you'll like this one."

"I'm all ears."

Mom takes a deep breath. I realize that she's excited. I can't remember the last time I've seen Mom really excited about something.

"Lark Austin is wooing me to be in her new film."

My jaw hits the floor.

"The Greek Mythology trilogy?" I say.

"Yes," Mom says. "She wants me to play Hera."

I nearly shit my pants, have a heart attack, bulge my eyes out of their sockets, and explode. Well, not really. But I might as well.

"*You? You* play Hera?"

In the Science Fiction and Fantasy Club, we have been trying to put a dream cast together for the Greek Mythology trilogy, and it has never, once, ever, included my mother in the role of Hera.

"Yes! We're still negotiating, but it looks real good," she says.

I can't believe it. My mom might actually be in something that I think is cool.

"Anyway. I've been invited to the premiere of her new movie at the Egyptian Theatre, and there's a reception, and I thought I would make you my date."

Mom's face is like the sun, big and hot and bright and happy.

"Saba Greer will be there, and I know how much you like her," she says.

This can't be happening. My mom can't actually start becoming cool.

"I'm already going," I remind her. "I volunteer at the Cinematheque. I'm working the reception. Jesus, Mom, take some notes or something. I live on this planet, too."

Mom's face falls. She thought she finally had the key to getting in with me. I think she thinks she's trying.

"Well, we can still make it kind of like a date. Won't that be fun?"

"I'll be there early."

"Oh. Well then," she says. "Okay."

I retreat down the hallway and go to my room and throw myself on my bed.

I turn and notice my masks staring at me. They sit on the shelf, passing judgment. They are grotesque and accusatory and I deserve it.

When I was a little girl, my mom and I were always laughing together and doing goofy things. We actually got along. Then, one day, we suddenly lost the ability to understand each other.

Despite my tough exterior, my I-don't-care attitude, my thick-skinned, slit-eyed meanness, I feel shitty about being horrible to my mom. She didn't do anything except try to be nice to me.

I discover that my cheeks are wet and I am crying.

Saturday. February 14. Lunchtime.
Trouble at Santa Land Set.

My prosthetic nose keeps dipping into the spoon and getting wet with vegetable soup. I told the makeup assistant person that I could take it off for lunch and put it back on by myself; I even told her I had the adhesive with me in my bag, but she didn't believe I could do it.

I told her that I thought the makeup guy was not as good as my dad. I told her that even I could do the special-effects makeup on this TV movie better than her. I told the producer of the show, too. But the producer refused to be influenced by me.

I hate all the other extras on the set, so I bailed on the free bagels and wraps and went to the commissary. Here at least I can read my book in peace and not talk to all the wannabes and weirdos that make up the background players.

I pull the nose off, meaning the makeup people will be upset with me, but fuck it. It's annoying to eat with, and I don't want to sip my soup through a straw.

I open my bag and take out my book, *The Stars My Destination,* and begin to read. I should study my math, but it's Saturday and for once I don't want to do homework.

After lunch, I head back to the set and into the makeup trailer to put my nose back on.

"Hello?"

They must all still be eating lunch. I make my way up into the empty trailer and run my hands along the countertop. I examine all the stuff. There's a clear tackle box full of ears. Another one full of noses. There are Styrofoam heads on shelves, with various latex parts pinned to them. The heads have the actors' names emblazoned on their foreheads in black Sharpie pen.

I close my eyes and listen to the sounds from the studio. The golf carts. The crackle of walkie-talkies. The extras, the actors, the crew walking by the open door of the trailer. I feel good in the makeup truck. Like I can breathe.

I motivate myself and rummage in my bag until I find the adhesive to secure my nose. Then I sit in the chair and begin applying.

"What are you doing in here?"

I look up into the mirror, and standing behind me is the head makeup guy.

"My nose came off."

"It shouldn't have come off."

"Okay, I pulled it off so I could eat my soup. I'm putting it back on."

"Did you go through my drawers?" he asks, motioning at the open drawer.

"Yeah, you used a different kind of adhesive from the one I have in my bag."

"Ah, you must be Victoria. Ursula told me about you."

He comes over and examines my work. Makes a slight color adjustment of the nose, blending in the edges. Then nods to himself.

"Good work," he says. Then he extends his hand. "I'm Jacques. I heard you were telling the producer you could do my job better than I can."

I feel kind of stupid hearing my words thrown back at me, but I look at him even-steven.

"I know how to do this. My dad taught me, and he is the best."

"I know who your father is. He's *one* of the best. I am another one of the best."

"Then why are you supervising makeup on a Movie of the Week?" I ask.

90

He stares me down. His face changes. Then it challenges.

"Grab the noses and ears and follow me."

"Really?" I say.

"Really. They've just called in thirty new extras and I could use a hand."

Sunday. February 15. 5:00 P.M.
Home.

On the dot, a car honks outside.

"Who's that?" Mom says.

"People," I say, and open the door.

"Where are you going?" Mom says. She's got a script in her hand. She's got a lot of scripts on the table next to her. She's been getting a lot of scripts lately.

"Out," I say, grabbing my keys and swinging out the front door.

"Victoria, when you . . ." but I don't hear the rest because I am already walking to the car.

Max's car is an old dark-green Ford Mustang. Of course it is.

Nelly is in the front seat. She smiles at me and waves. I can already see that I'm going to be in the back seat all night.

Nelly is wearing makeup, not just the peach-smelling lip-gloss she usually wears. She glitters. She glows. She looks great. I would want to kiss her if I were a boy. Max probably wants to kiss her. She is wearing a halter and a small shrug sweater. She must be wearing her contact lenses, because her glasses are nowhere to be found.

Max looks the same as usual. Black on black.

I am wearing my best Egg cloak, but I feel as though I'm underdressed.

"Let's go," Max says, and points the car toward downtown.

"So, downtown used to be way more sketchy than it is now," Nelly informs Max. She's smiling all the time. She jokes with him and slaps his knee or hits his arm playfully.

"Yeah, I know all about downtown," Max says gently to Nelly. "My dad's new documentary is about Los Angeles in the teens and twenties."

He obviously doesn't want to embarrass her. Max is not that careful with me.

"Oh," Nelly says. "Your dad makes movies?"

I can tell by the question that Nelly is always looking for her big break in Hollywood.

"I'm thinking about really seriously pursuing an acting career," Nelly says.

"He makes documentaries," I say from the back seat. "Maybe you've heard of them? It's nonfiction."

Nelly throws me a look.

I slump back into my seat, dark clouds forming over my head. I am already miserable.

"Yeah, documentaries," Max says.

"So you're almost nineteen?" Nelly asks, changing the subject tactfully.

"Yeah," Max says. "My parents travel a lot for their movies. I've traveled all over the world with them. I've lived in Africa, India, the Middle East, France. I've been to Russia, Mongolia, and New Zealand. I missed a year of school because of an embassy bombing."

"You were there?" Nelly asks.

"No," Max says. "But the school was closed."

"Is that where you got your scar?" Nelly asks.

I sit up. Scar? I never noticed any scar on Max Carter.

"What scar?" I ask.

"The one on his stomach," Nelly says.

Max glances at me in the rearview mirror. Our eyes lock. Then he looks back at the road. Nelly has seen Max Carter's stomach.

"No, I got that in Jerusalem." He doesn't need to say anything more about it.

"You've been all over," Nelly says.

"Not everywhere. Not Alaska. Not Antarctica. Not Tierra del Fuego," Max says. "How about you? Where have you been, Nelly?"

"Oh. Nowhere. Seattle. Tijuana. San Francisco. Phoenix," Nelly says. "I plan on traveling when I'm older."

94

"How about you, Egg?"

"My mom was on location and we went to Prague. I dunno, Tasmania once. And she did a commercial in Tokyo and I went."

"Ah, Tokyo," Max says.

"I don't understand," I say. "If you've been to all those cool places, why on earth would you decide to come to Melrose Prep?"

"I thought it might be fun," he says. "It's like a social experiment: a year of American high school in Hollywood. It was too good to pass up."

"Fun!" I snort. "If I had lived in all those places, I would just keep going. I would never let the dust settle on my shoes. Home is just a momentary place you need to rest your eyes."

"I told you, Egg. I'm an ethnographer. I'm interested in people," Max says.

Then he takes a sideways glance at Nelly, and it dawns on me that he's probably come to finish out senior year of high school just to meet girls.

"Well, I can't wait to get out of high school," I say.

"*Est unusquisque faber ipsae suae fortunae,*" Max says.

"Why do you do that?" I ask. "Latin is a dead language."

"Maybe it shouldn't be," Max says.

"Egg is only just sixteen," Nelly says, ignoring Max's annoying Latin.

"It doesn't mean I'm a baby. It means I skipped a grade," I say.

"Oh, that explains a lot," Max says, and turns on the radio. "You know, Egg, you look like a traveler."

It's a high compliment. I take it because Nelly wants it, and even though she's seen his stomach, Max gave the compliment to me.

"Yeah, I'm a traveler," I say with a laugh. It sounds like a tribe in a TV show or movie I might like. "Maybe I'll skip college and just travel."

"Really?" Nelly asks. This interests her and she turns around. She's behaving like a friend. "Are you serious? 'Cause my Dad flipped out when I told him that I don't want to go to college right away."

"Well, conveniently, I don't have a dad at home and I could care less what my mom thinks about my plans," I say.

I'm surprised I'm saying such things; it disregards everything I've ever felt about going to college. College has always been my goal, the one thing I've been sure of.

"Well, I'm going to take acting classes and go for it," Nelly says. "I mean, Hollywood is all about being young. I don't want to waste my young years in college. I can always go later."

I can see Max's shoulders tense up a bit. He pats his shirt pocket, which I know holds his small sketch-book. I know he's itching to write down what Nelly just said.

"I thought you were different, Nelly," I say. I almost admire her gumption.

"Yeah, well, *you* try being really smart *and* really pretty," Nelly says, insulting me without realizing it. "I mean, I want to win an Oscar, not a Nobel Prize. You know? And now that it's actually time to go to college, I'm not ready yet."

"How about you, Max?" I say.

"I've done my traveling for now. I want to settle down," he says. "I've never really had a group of friends. I want to know what that's like."

"You have like a billion friends at school," I say. "You talk to everyone."

"Yeah, I guess so," he says.

I notice that Max is grinding his teeth and that he looks like he wants to say more.

Nelly doesn't seem to notice anything out of the ordinary. She is looking out the window, eyes fixed on her own future.

"What are you trying to say?" I ask.

"I want to make my mark," he says.

But what target, I wonder, are you going to hit?

5:40 P.M.

Downtown Artspace.

Buns Not Guns Show.

The bass hits me right in the middle of my chest when we walk in the door of the Buns Not Guns show. We get X's on our hands demarking our under-twenty-one status and head inside to the art/performance space. It is in a loft on the ground floor of a huge old building that looks like it was used as the set of *Blade Runner*. Most of the windows on the upper floors are boarded-over or broken. Gentrification hasn't quite hit this side of downtown.

"Who are these people?" Nelly asks.

"They certainly don't go to Melrose," I say.

"Want some water?" Max says, raising his voice above the band.

I nod. It is easier than trying to be heard. Max heads off to the bar and I'm standing there with Nelly. She whips out her journalist's notebook and starts taking notes and giving me orders. She's moved from new-friend mode to overachiever-student-editor mode.

98

"I need you to get pictures of the bands and the art and the organizers," she says.

"I know what pictures to take," I say. "I don't need you to tell me."

"Well then, get your camera out and start snapping," she says.

She tugs on my camera strap. She probably means it to be friendly, playful. But to me it's aggressive. I bore a football-size hole in her head with my laser-adjusted eye.

Nelly removes her shrug and reveals her perfect, perky cleavage. That's when Max joins us again. I take my water from his hand. Max's eyes drift down to Nelly's breasts and then back up again. That puts me right in my place. Pretty on the outside wins over pretty on the inside. I want to go home and leave them alone, but I'm downtown and I don't want to take the bus home. I wouldn't even know which bus to take from here.

Mental note: Adventurers always know all bus routes and bus schedules.

"We should move up front, don't you think?" Nelly says, grabbing Max's hand and holding it and pulling him into the crowd up by the band, purposely leaving me behind.

I don't bother following them. I push away the feelings of being the third wheel. I remind myself that I am here on assignment.

I walk around and look at the art. It's very dramatic. I pick up the literature. It makes a lot of sense. I take a few pamphlets and stuff them in my bag. Then I take my camera out. Being a loner has its advantages when taking pictures. It allows you to get close up without ever being seen.

I shoot: The punk boys dressed in military camouflage. The shirtless lead singer with the self-cutting on his chest. The boy in drag. The tattooed couple. The piercings.

A boy with a kind of grown-out Mohawk, a knapsack, geek glasses, and tons of buttons on his suspenders comes up to me.

"What are you? Goth?" he asks.

"Post-apocalyptic," I answer.

"Cool," he says.

I snap his picture.

I find Max and Nelly in the crowd. Nelly is dancing provocatively and keeps taking Max's arm and trying to put it around her waist. He doesn't oblige her. But it looks like he might want to. It looks like he has before. I notice him turn and scan the crowd. Is he looking for me? I duck behind a pole so he doesn't catch me watching them.

Has he kissed her? Has he held those breasts?

People pushing to get closer to the stage jostle me. Even they don't see me. I'm invisible. I get it. I blend further into the crowd so I don't have to watch Max and Nelly anymore.

It's going to be a long night.

Wednesday. February 18. Free Period.
Student Quad.

I am sorting through a bunch of contact sheets, selecting the shots I want to blow up into prints.

So far, I like: The pile of elf ears. The production assistants sifting the snow from the rafters. My mother with a gruesome look on her face as she does her vocal warm-ups between takes.

I take the eyepiece magnifier and start on the second set. It's from the Buns Not Guns show. I mark a circle around a girl puking into the toilet in the crumbling bathroom. She looks so young, fresh-faced, like a baby. Her throwing up is like a coming-of-age story.

"What's this?" Max says.

"Contact sheets," I say, pointing out the obvious. I don't look up at him. I scan the next sheet.

"Can I look?" he says.

"Knock yourself out," I say.

"These are amazing," Max says.

I ignore the compliment.

"That warehouse space where the show was is an art gallery, too," Max says.

"I read their manifesto," I say. "It was kind of idealistic."

"At least it's an alternative to doom and gloom. It's *action*. The concept is simple. Buns. Not. Guns. It's something you can get behind," Max says. "I like the idea that you can provide *food* instead of *weapons;* it's something hopeful. I mean, I do stuff that sometimes seems like it's a big waste of time."

I'm intrigued. I look up from my eyepiece for a second.

"Like what?" I ask.

"I volunteer at the library to help a kid with his reading and math."

"The drop in the bucket theory," I say. "If everyone contributes a drop, then soon enough the bucket will be full."

"Exactly," Max says. "I knew you'd get it."

I look back at my contact sheet.

My eye hits an image of Max, magnified and just for me. He looks classic. Out of time. The picture could be from any era. He is looking right at the camera, right into the lens with those smart eyes. Behind Max is the blur of the crowd, moving like a frenzied mob, like an animal. In all that chaos his eyes managed to look right at me.

I don't circle the picture.

3:13 P.M.
Melrose Lion Meeting.
Ms. Dicostanzo is speaking too loudly to us. Nelly is whispering something to Max, who is doodling in his sketchbook. She keeps leaning closer and closer to him. Her chair might fall over.

I will it to fall over. I use my dormant mutant powers to force the chair to fall over. It doesn't.

Max has a smile on his face, but he's not looking at Nelly, just at the paper at the end of his black felt-tip pen.

"We really do have the most gifted staff this year. Bravo! Again!" Ms. Dicostanzo is clapping. She's a real positive-energy enforcer. She would be good to have in your army in the *Terminal Earth* future.

"Egg, this photograph is timeless."

She holds up the photograph of the underage girl throwing up in the bathroom with her peace patches on her bomber jacket.

"Thanks." I love it when I get compliments.

"But *this* is the cover." She holds up Max's political drawing of the girl throwing up in the bathroom with her bomber jacket full of patches like "Go! Green!" and "Peace on Earth" and "Buns Not Guns." At her feet is a six-pack of alcohol with labels like "Big Brother" and "Corporate Greed" and "War" and "Environmental Damage," then the puke coming out of her mouth forms the word "Hope" in perfectly small cursive.

It is exactly like the photograph I took, only it's politicized and cartoonified.

I have other pictures I took in this issue of the school paper, but that roll from the Buns Not Guns show, that roll was my favorite. It was the closest that I ever got to my heart. To my eye. To my voice. With that picture, it was as though I was finally learning how to speak.

Max looks up at me and mouths the words "I'm sorry."

I don't want to believe him.

11:09 P.M.
Cyberspace.

Knock, knock. Catburglar is trying to send you an instant message. Would you like to accept it?

Catburglar: I really liked those pictures from the Buns Not Guns show, Egg. You've really got a great eye.

Eggtoria: Yeah, so do you. Thanks for stealing my fucking picture, Max.

Catburglar: I didn't steal it. I just got so inspired when you showed me the contact sheets. It just summed everything up. Youth. Disillusionment. Despair.

Eggtoria: Well, that's the last time I show you anything of mine to get inspired by.

Catburglar: Don't do that.

Eggtoria: I'm mad at you.

Catburglar: You're mad at everything.

I don't respond. I continue surfing the Web. But Max doesn't give up.

Catburglar: Listen. I'm really, really sorry about the drawing I did based on your pic. I can talk to Dicostanzo about it.

Eggtoria: Whatever.

Catburgler: No. You have every right to be mad. Think of it as me paying you homage.

He sounds like he's being sincere. I still ignore him.

Catburglar: Don't stop showing me your contact sheets. Your eye is really inspiring to me.

Eggtoria: OK! I'm over it.
Catburglar: :)

I log off. Max Carter must be crazy. There is nothing inspiring about me, not even my GPA.

Friday. February 20. 6:00 P.M.
Egyptian Theatre.
A *Dream for the Moon* Screening.

The night of the screening is finally here.

I head through the courtyard to the guest-list table. Past the mountains of chocolate éclairs and pastry puffs. Past the table of baked Brie and crudités. Past the over-worn red carpet to Eduardo.

"Doors open in five minutes. I think it's going to be a madhouse." He points to the line already forming by the gate.

"Do you see Saba Greer anywhere?" I say.

"Oh, Lordy no!" Eduardo says. "Don't be crude! She's a whiskey. They don't wait in line."

"Whiskey?" I say.

"Yeah. They get whisked in," Eduardo says.

It must be an expression that he's made up and is hoping will catch on. I don't think it's going to work.

My mom is not a whiskey. She is standing in the line talking casually while signing an autograph for some stranger who has recognized her. She notices me at the desk and waves with her clutch purse. I look down at the guest list, pretending to be checking something important. I'm embarrassed for her. Maybe I should have whisked her in so she wouldn't be so obviously uncool in front of Lark Austin.

The security guard's walkie-talkie jumps to life with noise, and he gives Eduardo and me the okay to start letting people in. The people give us their names and we check them off the list and then they head straight toward the free booze and food.

When the line dwindles down to nothing, Eduardo dismisses me.

"Go," he says, waving me away with the back of his hand. "Go find your movie star or I'll never hear the end of it."

I wander into the courtyard full of people in black. All the ladies have blond streaks in their hair. They all wear glitter in their base to make them look sun-kissed. Their faces are frozen into one youthful expression from Botox injections. They look like they are so afraid to be themselves.

Then again, I guess if they were themselves they might be as lonely as I am. Maybe if I ever grow my hair out I'll run off and get blond highlights. That worries me.

I notice Saba Greer. She is being cornered by a

group of Eggophiles from the *Terminal Earth* message board. They all said they were going to meet her. They are all wearing those stupid white flowers.

I don't want to be like them. I don't want to meet those girls. I am so happy that I came here as myself. Not Egg. Just Victoria.

I notice that Saba Greer is not so much smiling while shaking their hands and signing autographs. She looks like she's cringing.

I see my mom and head over to her. I'm tired of standing alone. She is talking to a woman in a suit. The woman looks familiar. My mom stretches her arm out and waves her newly manicured nails and bangly bracelets at me. She hired a stylist for this evening.

She puts her arm around my shoulder.

"Lark Austin, I'd like you to meet my daughter, Victoria."

"Hi, Victoria, nice to meet you."

"Yeah, you too," I mumble looking at my feet.

"Victoria is a big fan of your movies," Mom says for me.

I nod. "Yeah. You're great. My favorite is *They Scream in the Night*."

"Thanks," Lark says. "I'm a big fan of your mom's. I'm excited that she's going to play Hera for me."

110

"Isn't that exciting? It's all settled! I wanted to tell you today but you were gone by the time I got back from signing the contracts," Mom says. She's drinking a glass of wine. Her glass has a large creamy-pink lipstick mark on it. I want her to notice it and wash it off. Everything about my mom is embarrassing me right now.

"I'll be right back; I've got to use the loo," Mom says. When in the Hollywood bubble land, she's always pretending to be British.

"Okay," I say.

"God, those girls with the white flowers in their hair are fucking pathetic."

I look up at the woman who is speaking. I can't take my eyes off of her. Flame-red hair flowing down her back. Face dotted with freckles. It's Saba Greer. It's Egg herself. I didn't have to go find her. She came and found me. It's perfect.

"I know, honey," Lark Austin says, slipping her arm around Saba Greer's waist. "But they're your bread and butter. They buy your action figure and keep you nice and pampered and pretty."

It's suddenly clear to me that they are a couple.

"But they're freaks," Saba Greer says. "I mean, they worship Egg. Those girls need to get a fucking life. Lonely. Pathetic. Pasty teenage girls."

She is talking about me. I try not to look as though I am lonely and pathetic and pasty. I try not to let on that I am one of those girls.

My heart sinks as I realize that Saba Greer is a bitch. I listen to her mouth off about her fan base for a while longer, and then I just stop listening to her altogether. She's an awful person. She's no hero.

"Who are you?" Saba Greer says, eyeing me suspiciously. "You're not an Egg freak, too, are you?"

"No, this is Ursula Denton's daughter, Victoria — right?" Lark says.

"Yes. Victoria," I say.

Saba Greer sticks her hand out to shake mine. I take her hand. Her grip is weak. Her hand is freezing cold and her skin is clammy. She is everything that Egg is not. I guess that's why they call it "acting."

"Pleased to meet you," she says. But she's not pleased at all. She's already looking behind me to see who else is here.

Wanda comes over to join us.

"Lark, Saba Greer. I see you've met our best intern and your biggest fan, Victoria."

Saba Greer and Lark shake their heads yes, that they have met me and I imagine probably immediately forgotten me.

112

"Well, we're going to start in about five minutes, so we should probably head inside," Wanda says.

"I'll help Eduardo break down," I say. They leave me standing there in the open air with my heart breaking. I look over at my mom's full glass of wine and down the whole thing in one gulp.

Then I notice a tray of full wineglasses that has been left on a table. I go over and take two glasses and down those as well. Then I take two more and wander off to behind a palm tree to drink in peace.

Saturday. February 21. 9:30 A.M.
Bed.

"How much wine did you have?" Mom says, standing in my doorway. She's yelling too loudly. My mouth feels like a cotton ball. My head is splitting right down the middle. This is my first hangover.

"Don't talk so loudly," I say.

"Excuse me?" Mom says.

"Please," I beg. I am actually begging my mom.

"Is this how you are going to behave at the *Nemesis* reception at the museum?"

"No," I say. "Please talk quietly. In fact, please don't talk at all."

"I give you so much freedom and this is what you do?" Mom says. "I didn't think that you would become a drunk."

Now she is making me angry. She is being dramatic, as usual.

"I'm not a drunk. I never get drunk."

"Except last night."

"Saba Greer was a bitch. She was a horrible, horrible *bitch*."

"Well, Saba Greer is playing Athena in the movie with me, and since you'll be coming with me to Greece this summer before you go to college, you'd better get used to her being a bitch."

"Maybe I'll have other plans for the summer," I say. "I'll be a high-school graduate and can make my own goddamned decisions about where I'll be this summer. I might not go to college right away. I might not even go at all. I'll be independent, and I would like to consider all the choices open to me."

Mom doesn't have an answer for that. She just slams the bedroom door shut.

I am so glad it's Saturday and not a school day.

I make my way to the bathroom and take some aspirin and drink lots of water. If I cared, I would notice that I look like hell.

I slide in front of my computer and log on to the *Terminal Earth* site. There are ten new postings all about the party at the Cinematheque last night. They all say that Saba Greer was the nicest, most sincere, most loving person ever and that she had complimented all of their Egg costumes.

That seals it. Saba Greer really *is* a good actress.

I follow a thread on the message board that asks the question, "Any chance Saba Greer is gay?" I'm tempted to reveal that I know she is dating Lark Austin, but I resist.

Monday. February 23. Lunchtime.
Student Quad.

"Well?" Rue is gooning at me, as always, trying to bond with me. "How was Saba Greer?"

"I thought you'd be swinging off the roof today," Martin says.

"It was so special," I lie.

I don't want them to laugh at me for worshiping someone who sucks.

Martin puts his arm around Rue's waist. It's so tender it makes me want to barf.

"Hey, Thursday, New Bev, *Lord of the Rings* marathon. Wanna come with us?" Martin asks.

"A bunch of us are going, and we're packing a picnic dinner," Rue says.

"Sure," I say. "I was going to go anyway."

I almost tell them that my mom is going to play Hera in the Lark Austin movie. But I don't. I know they really, really want to be the first people to know. They'll read about it online. They'll get the scoop soon enough.

I just don't want to do any more talking about it today.

3:06 P.M.

Dean of Students' Office.

"I don't know what to tell you, Victoria. You're really falling behind." Dr. Gellar has called me in for a special emergency meeting. She is actually worried about me. "You're an exceptional student, but—"

"It's not like I'm going to fail anything," I say. "I don't fail."

"Well, it seems as though you are really struggling with math this semester."

Dr. Gellar is trying to tell me that it's okay not to be perfect. I almost bring up the valedictorian question. But I don't. Because I don't really want to hear about it.

"I'll get a tutor. I'll catch up," I say. "I'm sure I can get someone to help me with trigonometry."

Dr. Gellar nods. "All your applications are in?"

"Yes, they're all in," I say.

"Good. Do you know where you want to go?"

"I haven't really decided about that yet," I say. "I have to wait until I see where I get accepted."

"Of course."

"Don't pull me out of the running yet, Dr. Gellar. I'm full of surprises."

"I know you are, Victoria," she says.

Tuesday. February 24. 5:03 P.M.
Sam Jurgen's Creature Shop.

"Don't forget. I'm going overseas for the next six weeks to prep for the new *Dracula* movie," Dad says.

Dracula. It's a big deal. All those vampires. All that blood. All those delicate bat wings and eyeballs and pointy teeth. He's been working hard on reinventing the way vampires look.

"Hey, Dad," I ask. "How did you know that you wanted to be a special-effects guy?"

"It was the one thing that made me happy," he says.

My heart skips a beat.

I pick up a piece of foam and start cutting it. I think best when my hands are working on a new project. All of a sudden, my mind is spinning at light speed.

This moment right here. Freeze time.

I am completely happy.

Wednesday. February 25. 7:00 A.M.
Melrose Prep Front Entrance.

"Hey, what's different about you today?" Max catches up with me in the school entrance. He's hurried up to me from the parking lot.

"Nothing. I'm exactly the same," I say.

"No. Something's different."

He looks me up and down. It's a little chilly outside this morning. His black sweatshirt is zipped all the way up and he has a knitted black ski cap on. His blue eyes water a little in the wind, making their color even more brilliant.

"Are you wearing makeup?" he asks.

"No."

"Did you dye your hair?"

"No."

I pull my new thrift-shop ski jacket closed as we cross the school courtyard.

"Hey," he says. Finally noticing. "Where's your cloak?"

"At home," I say.

Thursday. February 26. 1:37 A.M.
Cyberspace.

REUTERS: JAPANESE BIND SPINACH DNA TO SHEEP
A.P.: BOMB KILLS FOUR IN JERUSALEM
SCIENCE.COM: SUPERBUGS INVADING HOSPITAL

There is nothing but bad news.

The news has me convinced that an asteroid is going to hit the earth. That a bomb is going to go off in some city and that there will be a nuclear winter. That the sun will explode. That the moon will lose its orbit. That a plague will wipe the earth clean. That we will all starve from bad farming. That a volcano will erupt. That there will be a massive earthquake. That the polar ice caps will melt. That people are going to turn into zombies. That *they* are going to get us.

There is nothing I can do about any of it.

The only thing I can do is get good grades. I have control, ultimate control, over that. The only thing I can do is apply myself. Cannot fail. Must do well.

Mental note: Don't freak out.

122

1:20 P.M.
Study Hall. Library.

I push open the door to the library, and Rue is there holding court with her books. Her fedora is on the table in front of her, and her hair spills over her shoulders like a medieval queen. I make my way over to her.

"You know I get bummed out when you say you're going to come somewhere with Martin and me and then you back out at the last minute," Rue says. "You always do that."

She's referring to the *Lord of the Rings* movies.

"Nah, I'm not backing out—I am going to be there anyway."

"Oh, good!" she says. "So what's up?"

"I have to ask you a favor."

"A favor?" Rue says.

"Yeah. I need a math tutor. I'm having trouble with trig."

The light from the library window makes twelve triangles on the table. The size of the triangles is changed by the curves of the hat and the lines of the books.

I bite my thumb. Maybe she'll say no.

Instead, she wrinkles up her nose and purses her lips into a smile.

"I knew it! I knew one day you'd come to me for something!"

"So, you'll do it?"

"Yeah," she says. "How about here at one o'clock on Monday?"

"I'll be here," I say.

"I'm a real hard tutor," she warns me. "I expect a lot. I expect results."

"That's cool," I say. "I want to make the grade."

3:45 P.M.

Golden Apple Comics.

The waves of a minor earthquake. They bottom out. They roll. They undulate. They are like my feelings, only with little painful spikes in them. Those spikes are like the minute second of happiness that I feel when the sun shines just right. Or when the sunset looks a certain shade of pink. Or like this moment, when I am holding the shooting script to *Terminal Earth* in my hands.

"Looks good, doesn't it?" Martin says.

I really am excited, I say to myself. *I don't care if Saba Greer is a bitch. Egg still kicks ass. I still really like this movie.*

"It looks great. I can't wait to read it," I say, even though I know most of it by heart. "Zach Cross looks really hot in the pictures."

"So I hear Rue is going to help you with your trig," Martin says.

"Yeah, I'm struggling."

I'm too proud. It's embarrassing to admit I'm weak.

"It's okay, Egg. Everybody has an academic weakness. Mine is French. I can't conjugate worth shit, and you know those Ivy League schools like you to speak more than one language. As a scientist, I'll have to read texts and stuff in journals in other languages. But as hard as I try, I just don't understand French."

Why is it that when people try to make me feel better, it just makes me feel worse?

Friday. February 27. 10:37 A.M.
Free Period.

I head over to the *Melrose Lion* office and settle up with some photography stuff I have to hand in. I scan some pictures. I clean my camera. I sit and go through the assignment board and write down what I think I might be interested in shooting.

Nelly and Inez walk into the room. They nod in my general direction and then immediately forget that I'm there.

They start gossiping. Which I find boring.

"So anyway, we're at this café, it's called the King Kong Café, and it's all these supercool people. Adults, you know. Artists. College kids. There's this singer-songwriter on the stage. Anyway, it was a total scene. And Max starts to cough, and I'm like, 'Are you okay?' and he looks at me and he takes my hand and puts it up against his heart and says, '*Amor tussisque non celantur.*'"

I pop my head up and look over at them.

"What does that mean?" Inez asks.

126

"It means, 'Love, and a cough, are not concealed.' Isn't that romantic?"

"I think that's weird," Inez says.

"Then he told me all about his artwork that he's going to do. He's writing a whole novel with pictures."

"He's definitely weird."

I close the photography closet after loading up on Kodak paper. I don't want to hear any more. She can't actually believe that the feeling is mutual. She can't even find a cool café on her own. She doesn't even know the term *graphic novel*. She doesn't know Max.

Saturday. February 28. 2:30 A.M.
Cyberspace.

> *Catburglar: You up?*
>
> *Eggtoria: Yep. Are you?*
>
> *Catburglar: Ha ha. Your analysis of Dostoevsky's* Crime and Punishment *was really astute today.*
>
> *Eggtoria: Wow. A compliment from the literary king. I'm honored.*
>
> *Catburglar: A bunch of us were thinking of going to Griffith Park merry-go-round for a picnic Monday since it's a half day. Want to come?*
>
> *Eggtoria: I dunno. I wouldn't want to get in the way.*
>
> *Catburglar: ????*
>
> *Eggtoria: I'm tired, I'm going to sleep.*
>
> *Catburglar: The fresh air would do you good.*
>
> *Eggtoria: I said Good Night!*
>
> *Catburglar: Sweet dreams, weirdo.*

Sweet dreams. It blinks at me. It is a wish you make to someone you care about. It's something you say to someone special. You don't just say it to anyone.

128

Or do you?

Selectively, I ignore the word *weirdo* and I wrap the phrase *sweet dreams* around me like a security blanket. It is a blanket that will prevent any bad dream from visiting me tonight.

I sign off and lie in bed.

Monday. March 2. Zero Period.
Melrose Prep Front Entrance.

I push open the double door to school and get blasted by the heat of the hallway. Max follows as we enter AP Global History and take our seats.

I open my loose-leaf binder and take out my pen.

"That photo of the boys on the basketball team was hysterical," he says. "The way you framed it makes it look like some kind of cult meeting."

I notice that the line that goes from his neck and disappears down inside his hooded sweatshirt makes a beautiful curve. I am transfixed by the curve and the mystery of where it goes. I wonder what it would be like to kiss his neck. I wonder how the scar feels on his belly.

All of a sudden I'm very nervous.

I take out my textbook.

"Max, I really want to look at my notes before the exam."

"Okay, whatever." He turns his eyes to the front of the room and ignores me.

After a few minutes of staring at his back, the weird upheaval my body is experiencing settles down. I can breathe. I am back to normal.

I pull on Max's hood.

He turns around.

"I thought you were studying," he says.

He just thinks I'm acting normal. He can't tell that I am suddenly aware of every move, every sound, every word I make. He doesn't know that suddenly, everything I do or say sounds stupid. He doesn't realize what the word *sweet* has done to me.

"You still going to the merry-go-round today?"

"Yeah, you going to come?" Max asks.

"Yeah," I say, trying not to look abnormal. "Okay."

12:10 P.M.
School Parking Lot.
Nelly is leaning on Max's car. She waves.

"Hey, Egg," she says; then she turns to Max. Head sideways. Knowing look.

"Hey," she says to Max. Her arm loops under his. "I've got good news and bad news. What do you want first?"

"Bad news," he says, chewing on a fingernail.

Nelly looks at me and then at Max.

"I can't go with you to Griffith Park."

"And the good news?" Max asks.

"I got a callback on an audition!"

He unhooks her arm from his and unlocks the door and opens it.

"Hey, that's great," Max says. "What kind of movie is it?"

"Oh, it's not a movie," Nelly says.

"What is it then?" I say.

"An acne commercial," Nelly says.

I focus in on Nelly's face. Nelly's skin is perfect. She has no pores. No acne. No blemishes. They must want her to be the after picture.

"It's a national!" Nelly says, and crosses her fingers.

"Wow!" I say with mock enthusiasm.

"Hucking for the man, huh, Nelly?" Max says. "That's really . . ."

"What?" Nelly says.

"It's just not . . . It's just so corporate. It's doing something for the money and not because you believe in it. I mean, do you even care about the product?"

"It's just a commercial, Max. It's just a job," Nelly says.

I know Nelly is not stupid, but I can't believe she doesn't get what Max is saying.

"I wish you'd understand," Max says. "It's what's

destroying the truth and beauty of the world. Advertising. I mean, you don't even have acne."

"Look, Max. I get what you're saying. I just don't think it's that big a deal. I want to be an actress. I have a callback for a job. It's that simple."

Max gets a sullen look on his face that I've never seen before.

"Come on, don't be like that." She makes a cute face. "Call you later, okay?"

Max moves away from her slightly.

"Okay," Max says.

"No hard feelings?" Nelly asks.

"Nah," Max says, and gets behind the wheel. "Congrats on the commercial."

Does Max like Nelly so much that he will even compromise himself for her? I wonder if that's what caring is all about. If it is, I'll never care for anyone.

Nelly picks up her bag and leaves. She doesn't care that I'm going to the park with Max, because she's not threatened by me as a girl. She thinks I'm like Max's little pocket pal.

"Come on, Egg. Looks like it's just you and me."

I'm afraid to be alone with Max Carter. Not because he's scary, but because he's so real.

Griffith Park Merry-Go-Round.

I sit on the horse as it spins on its track. Around and around. Up and down. Max Carter's mouth is wide open next to me in a smile. His steed is purple. He is standing up. Fist in air. Triumphant. He slaps his purple horse's ass to make it go faster. But it is constrained by the bar, by the machine, by the mechanics, by the circle it is endlessly forced to travel in.

The ride stops.

"Again!" Max whoops.

We give our tickets to the ticket taker and we ride again. An endless circle. A sure journey. The music piping us back in time.

I am so happy that if this were a movie, a nuclear bomb would explode right now, ending my life in a perfect fireball.

We sit down on the grass apart from everyone else. Max pulls out a baguette, some cheese, and cold cuts so we can make our own sandwiches. There is also some bubbly water.

"This is very fancy," I say.

"Really? It's just bread and cheese," Max says.

"Well, the presentation."

"Oh. I figured it would be easier. I didn't know what you or Nelly liked."

He fixes himself a sandwich. He's not shy about it. He just heaps the Brie onto the bread.

"You're a pretty comfortable person, aren't you?" I say.

Max looks at me, head sideways.

"Yeah. Is there any other way to be? I mean, this is it. This is my body, my soul; I gotta live with it. I'd better get comfortable. I plan on taking it for a long ride," he says.

I laugh.

"The truth is I feel awkward around people sometimes," Max says. "I'm really quick to jump into being friends with people, 'cause, you know, I traveled so much growing up. I don't know how to be friends with people for more than a few days or a few months."

"You seem to be doing fine," I say, not wanting to admit that I envy him his social ease.

"Well." He motions over to the group we came to the park with but are not associating with at all. "I made friends with all of them, but I don't know if I actually like them. For real. Most of the time I still feel lonely."

This blows me away. I don't know what to say, so I open my mouth and put my sandwich in it to stall.

"I envy you, Egg. You're truly comfortable with yourself," Max says.

"No, I'm not," I say.

I want to tell Max that I am uncomfortable all the time, too. I need to hide myself. I need to hide my face. I need to hide my body. But I don't say it out loud. I almost think he wouldn't laugh at me for saying what I feel. I almost think I could trust him.

"Anyone who dresses up like a character from a movie and wears a cloak to school is pretty comfortable with herself," Max says.

"I'm not," I say.

"You are, too," he says.

"I'm not."

"You are, too."

We laugh like little kids.

"You really like yourself, Egg," Max says. "Deep down inside. That's what I like about you. You're really true to yourself. I try to be like that."

I take another bite of my sandwich. The lemon mayonnaise springs my taste buds to life.

"What's up with you and that *Terminal Earth* movie, anyway? I mean, it's a good movie. But it's not a great movie."

"It's pretty great," I say.

"But not *that* great," Max says.

"You know, Max. I've always been perceived as strange for one reason or another. I guess it's because of my overflowing amount of knowledge. Nobody seems to get what I'm talking about, so I just don't talk," I say.

"I know about that," Max says. "I call it loneliness."

I notice that the natural highlights in Max's hair are slightly reddish.

"Yeah. So everyone always thought I was strange or weird or something out of the ordinary, but not in a good way. *Terminal Earth* actually put all that knowledge to use for once. It just means something important to me," I say.

"I understand that. I even admire that," Max says. "I just don't get why you put all your knowledge and energy and passion into something like a movie. That's not real, you know? And there is this whole world around you, a real one, that's falling apart. That you could do some good in."

"Like march on the convention center," I say.

"Yeah, or help a kid to read or do algebra. Get people to vote."

"How does that really help?" I say.

"One person at a time. Many voices joined together become strong and loud," he says. "Like you said, a drop in the bucket."

"I don't have that much faith in people. I think the human race is going to self-destruct," I say.

"You should have more faith. People, in general, are good."

"You're so holier-than-thou," I say. "I'm irritated now."

Max laughs. "That's what my dad says."

"Besides, Zach Cross is hot."

Max laughs again.

The kids on the merry-go-round are screaming with joy as they whip around on their horses. The horses make a soft blur from where we are sitting on our grassy knoll. The birds. The sun. The outside.

"I watched my dad interview Zach Cross once," Max says. "Every time Zach Cross said something he thought was stupid, he would punch his own head."

"What do you mean, he beats himself up?" I ask.

"I mean he punches his head and yells at himself."

"That's not true," I say.

"And he's a drunk."

"No," I say.

"And he's gay."

"Shut up, Max. According to the *National Enquirer,* my mom is gay."

We are silent for a while. I am lost in my own thoughts. I always said that *Terminal Earth* wasn't just a phase. It wasn't just another thing that I was obsessed with that I'd later discard. *Terminal Earth* would be forever. And yet, I have gotten rid of Egg's cloak. And I don't really care anymore what happens in the sequel.

I just want to pass trigonometry.

Max reaches out his hand and smudges my lip with his thumb.

"You had some mayo on you," Max says.

His blue eyes are glinting in the sun. His smile, warm and large, is disarming. I look down at the grass. I feel naked. An army of ants is moving one of the bread crumbs at my feet to an unknown destination.

Tuesday. March 3. 6:58 A.M.
Student Quad.

I run up to Max as he emerges from the parking lot into the quad.

"Hey, there's a four P.M. special screening at the Silent Movie Theater that I was thinking of going to after school. Do you want to go with me?" I ask.

Dad is out of town. I have the afternoon to myself.

"Oh, man. It's *The Four Horsemen of the Apocalypse*, right? I saw that on the marquee on the way to school. Shit," he says.

"What's the problem? Tutoring kids? Bringing meals to sick people? Volunteering at an old-age home?" I say. "Don't save the world—come and hang out with me!"

"Can we take a rain check? I promised Nelly that we would do something today, you know, just us, and I don't think she'd want to go to the Silent Movie Theater," he says.

"So what? Blow her off," I say, irritated that he'd blow me off for her.

"I can't. I promised her," Max says.

140

"So what? I am way more interesting."

"Egg, Nelly and I are, you know . . . *hanging out.*"

It's like a push. It's like a slap. It's like I've had the wind knocked out of me. But I don't want Max to see how much it hurts.

"God, Max, I thought you were different," I say it cool, even, like a hiss between my teeth. "Nelly doesn't even appreciate the things that you talk about."

"Nelly's a great girl. She's smart. She's pretty," Max says. "I like that she's different from me."

"But she's typical," I say. "She's normal."

"She's not normal."

"Say she's just one of your social experiments. Say that you're studying her."

"No. She's not an experiment," Max says.

"I thought you liked exceptional things. Like me."

"I do," he says. "I do like you. But . . ."

"But I'm boy proof."

"No," Max says. "You just make yourself so unapproachable. And Nelly doesn't."

The worst thing is that what he's saying is true. It is difficult to discover that the truth really does hurt.

My body tenses up. I slam my locker door shut. The textbooks inside jump and clang on the thin metal shelf. The mini-comic from the *bande dessinée en directe* that I had taped to the door flutters to the floor.

"Come on, Egg. Don't be like this."

"I let you in," I say, "because I thought you liked me."

I head for AP Global History.

"I do like you," Max says, following me. "That's why I thought I could be honest with you. Egg, I'm not interested in tiptoeing around someone's feelings."

But *I* can't be honest with Max. I don't say what I really want to say, which is I thought that Max Carter liked me, like a girl, like I was pretty and special.

I can't even see in front of me, I'm so upset.

I get into the classroom, and the early sun's light crosses in lines that make me angry. I slide in behind my desk and slouch into my chair and fume. I try to think about something that makes me happy, but nothing springs to mind. It is all overpowered by my feeling like an idiot for thinking even for half a second that I liked Max or for stupidly thinking that maybe he liked me back. I can't believe I got myself thinking that it was something real. It drives me insane that I would lose to some girl like Nelly.

Girls like Nelly always win.

I'm always going to be invisible.

Max turns around in his chair to face me. I lean over and pretend to dig something out of my bag.

"Don't turn your back on me," Max says.

"I'm not. I'm looking for something."

"Egg . . ."

"Oh, God! Now I get it," I say. "'Love, and a cough, are not concealed.' That is so fucking lame!"

"You knew that something was going on," Max says. "You never brought it up, either."

"I didn't want to believe it," I say.

"Why is this such a big deal?" Max says.

"Why didn't you tell me? You should've told me. Instead of leading me on."

My heart is bursting. I feel savage.

"I didn't lead you on," Max says defensively.

"Right."

He stares me down, hoping I'll back off. Hoping I'll let him get away with it.

"I guess I didn't want to have that conversation," Max says quietly. "It seemed complicated."

"There's nothing complicated about it," I say. "You're just another shallow person pretending to be deep."

Max takes out his sketchbook and places it on the corner of his desk like he always does.

"I can tell you want to sketch something. I can see you want to retreat into that little book of yours. So why don't you just sketch me doing this," I say, and I lean over the desk and pour my latte on the sketchbook. "Try putting that in your stupid graphic novel."

Max jumps up and grabs his sketchbook like it's an injured child and mops the coffee up off the page with his sweatshirt sleeve. I can see some ink running, but I can tell the damage is not as much as I'd like it to have been. It doesn't match how I feel.

So I add words.

"I bet your graphic novel will suck. I bet it's typical, boring, and pedantic, just like you."

"Fuck you," Max says. It doesn't surprise me. What surprises me is how still he is when he says it. "You're angry all the time, Egg. You don't let anyone in. I don't know why. It's obvious that you have a spark, a passion, a heart. You have so much potential to be a fantastic person and you just choose to piss it away."

Max is calling me on my shit. I'm just a big baby and I can't stop being angry. I can't stop to listen to what Max has to say because everything he is saying is right.

Max closes his eyes and breathes deeply and then turns away from me. Now it's obvious that Max has decided not to try to say anything to me anymore. And I know I've ruined my life.

Mr. Gerber enters the class. I want to switch my seat. I want to run out of the room.

Max's back is held still but with lots of energy. I can see it flowing off of him. It's making me uncomfortable.

Mr. Gerber unfastens the buckles on his briefcase and gets the exam out.

"Max Carter, hand out these exams."

Max grabs the papers and hands them out to the class. When he gets to my desk, he throws my exam at me.

I want to melt into my chair and disappear. I want to punch a hole right through the floor. I don't want to think about Napoleon Bonaparte. I'm having my own private war.

Lunchtime.

Alone on My Bench.

Groups around me squawking their gossip.

Black, black cloud surrounding me.

I look up from my burrito hopefully. Maybe it's Max. Maybe I'm going to talk to him about how fucked up I am and how stupid I am.

It's not Max. It's Rue, and she has her hands on her large, wide hips.

"Where were you yesterday? I waited forever for you in the library."

"What are you talking about," I say.

"You had an appointment with me. To do trigonometry," Rue says.

"Oh, shit. I totally forgot."

"Well, I was stuck in the library waiting for you for two hours, on half day."

"It can't have been a big deal. I thought you spent all of your time in the library anyway."

I can hear the meanie inside of me just coming out. I don't even have any control over it. I want everyone to feel as bad as I do.

Rue's face falls. It slides down off her head and hits the floor. Hard. I didn't even mean to do it.

"Is that what you think? That I don't have a life? That I'm a big nothing that can wait around for you? You're mean and ungrateful, Egg. I have tried and tried to be friendly to you, but you just push me away all the time," she says.

I don't answer, because it's true. Everything she is saying is right on target. Today I am taking an emotional beating.

"You know what? Figure your own shit out." Rue starts walking away from me. Then she suddenly turns back toward me and shoves some papers into my hands.

"Here's some sample problems I wrote down for you. Don't ask me for any more help. Don't talk to me. Don't try to apologize."

She's crying now.

I've broken her. Her nose is running freely and

catching on the kewpie-doll lips she has. Her pale skin blotches red all over. It's as if she's suddenly sprouted hives. She takes her scarf and dabs her eyes with the corner of it. She's the kind of girl who's nice and helpful even when she's angry and upset. She's the exact opposite of me.

I see something I've never seen in her before. I see a rare beauty. I am itching to pull my camera out of my bag and take a picture of her, but I don't dare. She would never understand. She would think I was making fun of her.

Rue turns herself around and disappears down the hallway.

That's two people I've pissed off today. And it's only fifth period.

2:25 P.M.
In the Darkroom.
The red work light tempers me. I am messing everything up. Nothing is going right. I want to cry.

The photographs magically appear in the developer. I poke at them with the tongs. Another student comes in through the revolving door of the darkroom. It's Max Carter.

"We have to talk," he says. The red light eliminates all the hard features from his face. He looks smooth and unreal. I wonder if I look the same.

"No, we don't," I say, because I am afraid of what he'll say to me. I'm afraid of what I'll say to him. I'm afraid I'll say that I am so glad that he's come to Melrose Prep and that I'm so glad that I have a friend.

"I've been doing a lot of thinking . . ." Max says.

"Shut up," I say.

"No," Max says.

But he does shut up, because I turn my face away from him and I don't say anything, and so the silence is frozen between us.

Max just stands there. I think it's a relief that maybe he will just go away and I can just be alone, like I was before. Even though truly, I don't want him to leave.

After what seems like ten lifetimes, Max exits the revolving door back out to the light. Leaving me by myself in the darkroom.

I push open the door to the Science Fiction and Fantasy Club meeting. Everyone stops their chatter when they see that it's me. Rue looks away from me. She looks at the wall. Martin is shaking his head. I know she's told everyone that she has had enough of me.

It's obvious that no one wants me there. Hasan is the only one brave enough to say anything.

"You kept valuable information from us, Egg," Hasan says. Clearly he's hurt. "Our club mantra is to share all insider information on the films and television shows that we talk about."

"I know. I helped make up the rules," I say.

"Well then, you also know that you are officially suspended for keeping information to yourself," Hasan informs me.

I can tell he's embarrassed that he has to spell this out to me, because his slight lisp is more pronounced.

"What are you talking about?" I say.

"We know your mom is playing Hera. It was

149

announced today, and we all figure you've known for a while," Martin says. "Sorry. You know the rules. You're suspended from the club until you can bring us a worthy piece of insider information."

"This is bullshit," I say. "It's my mom. It's different."

"It's the rules we all agreed on together," Mr. Padilla says. He's sorry, too. I can tell. But he's not going to stand up for me.

"How about a scoop like Saba Greer is dating Lark Austin?"

"Old news. It's already all over the Web," Martin says. "Somebody posted it on the *Terminal Earth* message board."

"Besides, outing somebody is cheap," Rue says. "And it doesn't pertain to film information."

"Whatever," I say. "I'm cheap, I'm mean, and I'm a waste." I push open the door and get the hell off campus.

Thursday. March 19. 9:16 A.M.
The Hallway Between Classes.

Still no one is talking to me.

A month ago this would have been preferable. Now it is torture.

The days get measured by the things that don't happen anymore. Like Max's head never turns in my direction to say something clever. Rue never pats the empty seat next to her at lunchtime.

There are more alien and monster doodles than notes and homework assignments written in my loose-leaf binder.

I haunt the hallways like a broken spirit.

7:10 P.M.
Museum of Television and Radio.
The Nemesis Cast and Crew Reunion.

My mom is not embarrassing me. She's actually being totally cool. I've never seen her as anything but washed up. But tonight, she looks gorgeous. Her hair is in an upsweep, with some glitter in it for a sparkling effect. She's wearing a fabulous new dress with jewels on loan. How she shines in the light of the paparazzi. How she glows as she walks down the red carpet. How she smiles with genuine happiness and squeezes my hand and says to me in a whisper, "This is it, baby. I'm back on top."

I guess I never paid attention. It really means that much to her being an actress. She really is a star.

But me, I'm nothing. I'm a black hole.

Hasan is by the stinky cheese table, ignoring me. I look him over—sloping shoulders, large stomach, man breasts. His body language tells me that he wants to talk to me. He widens his eyes at me, like an alien.

"How did you guys get in?" I ask Hasan. I genuinely want to know. I'm glad they're here. I'm glad for the familiar, if unfriendly, faces.

Hasan looks over to the group of my former acquaintances. Rue slits her eyes at me like a cat. Martin shakes his head. A few others from the Science Fiction and Fantasy Club turn around, physicalizing the cold shoulder they are collectively giving me.

"Well, it was no thanks to you," Hasan says.

"I know," I say. "I'm sorry. I mean it. For real."

"Rue's dad got us in," Hasan says, and finishes

loading up his plate with a small mountain of bread, cheese, and olives.

I suddenly wish that I had invited them. I wish that I had not been such a tightass with my in at the event. These are the only people I know who can appreciate some of the things that I like, and I miss them.

"I miss talking to you guys. You guys are my friends. What if I said I was sorry, Hasan?" I ask.

"It would help if you really meant it," he says.

I see an opening here. I can see Hasan wanting to crack. He wants to tell me it will be okay. But then he moves away from me to rejoin the true friends he came here with tonight.

Saturday. March 21. 8:15 P.M.
Gogo Sushi. Little Tokyo.

Saba Greer blinks too much. I never noticed that she blinked that often in *Terminal Earth*.

"Can I try one of those halibut sashimis?" she asks me sweetly.

Saba Greer is kissing up to me to get on my mom's good side. It's so strange. Once upon a time, this would have been a dream come true. But now that Saba Greer is just a normal person and not a hero who saves humanity from itself at the end of the world, it's just a bummer.

"Knock yourself out," I say, and push the tiny plate with the halibut roll over to her side of the table.

"Thanks," she says. Blink. Blink. Blink. Blink.

God, it is so annoying. I blink back at her, but she just smiles. She doesn't realize that I am making fun of her. She's such an idiot. I suppose they must have digitally erased her eyelids in *Terminal Earth* in order to

154

make her look less annoying. They can fix just about any imperfection in the movies.

Imperfections. I sum them up.

Saba Greer blinks too much in real life. My mom has a chip in her tooth, and Lark Austin's hair is thinning.

And me, I'm ground zero for my own personal apocalypse.

"Would you like to try the eel?" I say politely. My mother smiles because I'm making an effort to join in the conversation. But I just really hate eel.

"You know, Saba, the tabloids said *I* was gay once," my mom says between bites of squid.

"But you're not gay," Saba Greer says. "Besides, they got it wrong. I'm not gay. I'm bi."

"One of those Eggophiles posted it on the *Terminal Earth* message board," Lark Austin says.

"I was going to do a whole spread of coming out in *The Advocate*," Saba say. "It was going to be a great publicity thing for me. But now that's ruined because of the tabloid thing. I hate not having absolute control over what's said about me."

"It's still great publicity. We can spin it any way we want," Lark says. "It's giving me great buzz for the Greek Mythology trilogy."

"Well, it's just about damage control now," Saba

155

Greer says. "What pisses me off is that the tabloids keep outing Zach Cross and it never affects him."

"Well, you know what they say. When a door is closed, a window opens," Mom says.

Mental note: Time to rethink my life. Time to look for that window.

Wednesday. March 25. Last Period.
AP English.

It's been four weeks since Max Carter has spoken to me. He doesn't answer my instant messages. He's right in front of me in Global History class every day and he never once turns around to chat with me anymore.

I always *thought* I was lonely, but now that no one is talking to me, I really know what lonely is.

In English class, Max is still sitting right next to me. I can smell him. I think he smells good. I want to reach over and touch his arm and make him turn to look at me. But no matter how much I jiggle in my seat and make noise, he just keeps looking straight forward.

Today, I swear, I am going to fix it. I am going to say something.

"Can I borrow a pen? Mine is out of ink," I say.

Max doesn't answer. He continues working on his essay.

"Max, please talk to me."

Max doesn't answer. He's hesitating, though. I'm wearing him down.

"Max, I'm really sorry," I say. I really am sorry. I miss Max Carter. I miss my old loner life. The one that was full of people.

He leans back on his chair and dips his hand into his bag and gets me a pen. He still doesn't say anything. But it feels like progress.

The only way that Jacques will let me continue helping him out with the makeup is if I continue on as an elf extra. My one-day elf stint has stretched into over a month of after-school work. Good for the wallet and good for my makeup training. It's the only thing that is keeping me sane now that no one is talking to me.

I cut out of the set for *Trouble at Santa Land* and head toward the commissary for dinner break.

I have to do my homework.

I order a latte from the girl behind the counter and then sit down and look at the math problems I've been assigned. They don't make any sense to me. The numbers blur in front of me. I have coffee rings on my loose-leaf paper. Instead of doing my homework, I begin to trace out dinosaurs and flying saucers with my pencil.

I'm thinking. I'm thinking. I don't know what the answer is. I need help. I fucked up badly when I lost Rue as my tutor. I'm so stupid. I have no one to turn to and it's my own fault. I'm all on my own. I'm not as smart as I always think I am.

I sip on my latte. I'm buzzed from all the caffeine. I'm trembling and quivery inside. I want to concentrate on the proof.

All I can think about is how I'm going to fail trigonometry. I've definitely lost my spot as valedictorian. At this point, I'll probably have to go to summer school. I'm not going to get into a good college, and I'm never going to show Max Carter or anyone else that I can be friendly.

I must be crazy. I'm talking to myself.

Too much coffee has made me have to pee. I go to the ladies' room and relieve myself and then, to torture myself, I order another half-caf latte.

On my way back to the table, I see a tall, dark man leaning over my notebook, scribbling in it.

"Hey!" I yell. "Hey there, what are you doing?"

The man turns around and looks at me. I move toward him in slow motion, in disbelief. My brain is frozen, but my feet know what to do. They keep moving.

It's Zach Cross. It's Uno. Zach Cross from *Terminal*

Earth has been scribbling in my math notebook. My feet move me back toward my table and I sit down.

"I just found the mistake you made," Zach Cross says to me.

"What?" I say.

"You see, you used the wrong table here. That's why you're off," Zach Cross says. He looks at me sideways, suddenly noticing my costume. "What are you?"

"I'm an Awkwardly Tall Elf," I say. Then I jingle the bell on top of my hat.

"Oh," he says. "Cool."

Then, undistracted by my ridiculous costume, probably because he has worn more ridiculous getups than mine, he helps me with my trigonometry homework.

"Oh!" I say after about twenty minutes. "I think I get it."

He smiles. He is more beautiful in person than in the movies. He punches my shoulder, like we're friends.

"I thought you were in New Zealand," I say.

"I am. I had to come back and do some looping for my last film," he says.

"Are you gay?" I say.

"What?" Zach Cross says.

"Everyone says you're gay," I say. "I don't care if you are. It's no big deal."

"I'm not gay," he says.

"Are you stupid?" I say. "'Cause that's another thing everyone says as well."

He sets his mouth into a grim line. He furrows his brow. He turns his perfect movie-star eyes on me, and says, "I'm not a man of many words, but I understand math."

"Saba Greer is dating Lark Austin," I say.

"You can't believe what the tabloids say," Zach Cross says.

"I met them at the Cinematheque with my mom," I say. "They were holding hands."

I lean back on my chair and nibble on the piece of cake that Zach Cross has bought me, and something dawns on me.

"Hey, Zach," I say. "I've got a problem that you can help me solve."

"More math?"

I explain to him what happened with the Science Fiction and Fantasy Club and my holding back on my mom being Hera in the Greek Mythology trilogy. "So, I need some inside dirt on *Terminal Earth*," I say.

"Your mom is Ursula Denton?" Zach asks.

"Yeah," I say. "I'm Victoria."

I don't say I'm Egg.

"I had your mom's poster on my wall when I was a

kid. I was in love with her," he says. "I'll dish the dirt for you. You can share with your friends, but you didn't hear it from me."

Then Zach Cross begins to tell me some gorgeously heavy secrets about the new *Terminal Earth* movie.

Wednesday. April 1. 7:04 A.M.
On the Way into School.

A homeless man sleeps outside of the school every morning. Sometimes I give him change. Or I give him an apple. Or I give him a mean, awful look and say, "Go away."

But today, something seems different. Normally he is an invisible citizen. But today, his dirty face reminds me of those birds slicked with oil.

I take my camera out of my bag and take his picture as he shuffles off with his blanket. I capture him as he carefully unhooks his dog from the bench that he calls a bed every night. I follow him as he panhandles for some change that might bring some food to his belly or some wine to his surely rotting gut. I focus on his blackened fingernails and yellow teeth. His scarred face. His over-sunburned arms. His gentle eyes. His wild, peppered, dark hair. His missing tooth.

I bring the proof sheet into the *Melrose Lion* meeting.

Max Carter looks up at me as I enter the meeting. Nelly has her head leaning on his shoulder. I can imagine that this is the way she places herself on him after wrestling with him on the bed.

I push an envelope of photographs that I took that morning toward the center of the table.

"I brought something in," I say. "I thought we could use it as a social commentary piece."

"Max and I do commentary," Nelly says. Nelly has become as frigid toward me as everyone else has. Her nice-girl skills only extend so far.

"I didn't write a story. I took some pictures," I say.

I push the envelope into the middle of table. Max starts to reach for it.

"Maybe we should take a look," Max says.

My chest tightens with a hopeful feeling.

"I'm student editor. I have final word," Nelly says, turning to me with those smart eyes of hers. "Just hand in what we ask you to."

Ms. Dicostanzo sweeps into the room.

"Sorry I'm late. The traffic is so horrible since they've started widening all the streets in Hollywood," she says.

Everyone looks at me. They all know I could play the Dicostanzo card. I could force Nelly to look at my proof sheet. I could get her to consider accepting

165

something for the *Lion* that wasn't planned. We all know we're supposed to work as a team.

I pull my manila envelope back and stuff it in my bag.

"Did you share something with the group?" Ms. Dicostanzo asks me.

"Nah, it was nothing," I say.

Mental note: Always know when to keep big mouth shut.

Out of the corner of my eye I almost notice that Max is about to speak up for me.

But then again, maybe it's just wishful thinking.

Thursday. April 2. 8:32 A.M.
In the Hallway.

New tactic: Be friendly.
I smile big and I say hello to twelve people today in the hall.

"Hello, Rue."

"Hello, Martin."

"Hello, Hasan."

"Hello, Nelly."

"Hello, Max."

"Hello, Katrina."

"Hello, Damon."

"Hello, Jessica."

"Hello, Ignacio."

"Hello, Tamara."

"Hello, Sid."

"Hello, Christina."

No one says hello back. But I don't care.

Mr. Padilla's Physics Room.
Science Fiction and Fantasy Club Meeting.

"You're not welcome," Rue says.

"Yeah," Hasan says.

"According to the bylaws of our club, I can return as a member in good standing if I supply a piece of information as good as the one I withheld."

Martin looks up from his copy of *F/X* magazine. I have captured his attention.

"Technically, yes. But in this case we won't accept any inside information from the Greek Mythology trilogy," he says.

Everyone mutters in agreement. Mr. Padilla wants me back in the club, I can tell. He waves his hands like a conductor for everyone to sit down and come to order. Then he motions for me to enter the room.

"Let's hear what Egg has to say," he says. This makes me smile.

"I have insider information on *Terminal Earth*," I announce.

"No go, Egg," Martin says. "We all know that they are shooting parts two and three back to back."

"Yeah," Rue says. "And we all know that there is a superhighway chase in Tachon City. Martin downloaded the pictures from the Internet two days ago."

Martin raises his finger in the air to present himself as if I don't know that it's him.

"Okay, but do you know that Uno has a sister, who he finds in the abandoned city of Tachon?" I say.

I could have heard a pin drop in the room.

"And do you know that Egg's child was buried at the beach at Konkar and that she can never have a child again because she was one of the only people that survived the white plague in its first incubation?

"And did you know that Uno is going to save his unborn child with a new female character named Trillia, but not without a great personal sacrifice?"

"Where did you hear all of this?" Rue asks in disbelief.

"I can't say. My sources are confidential."

"We need to verify it, Egg. You know the rules."

"You can't verify this," I say. "You won't find it anywhere, and I could get into big trouble. It's not going to hurt anyone, but it could spoil some people's fun, so let's keep it between ourselves."

Everyone in the room looks at each other. They know everything I say makes complete sense, but rules are rules.

"Well," Mr. Padilla says. "What should we do?"

He's really asking the club, not me, but I answer for everyone because I belong here, with my friends.

"You should trust me," I say.

Rue smiles at me and begins to clap her hands. Hasan and Martin join in and then the rest of the club members do, too.

"Welcome back, Egg," Martin says.

"You know, my real name is Victoria," I say, and it feels good. My name is Victoria. It's a comfortable fit.

Monday. April 6. 3rd Period.
Dean of Students' Office.

My mother has never ever had to come to school to
meet with anybody about my grades, but now that it is
certain that I am failing trigonometry, Dr. Gellar needs
my mother to come in.

"What an honor it is to meet you, Ms. Denton. My
husband has been a longtime fan of yours. As a boy, he
had your poster up in his room."

I make a small, quiet gagging noise. My mother
shoots me a look.

Dr. Gellar, now reduced in my eyes to yet another
starstruck dork, hands my mom a Sharpie pen and her
husband's childhood poster of her in a swimsuit. My
mom, with whom flattery goes everywhere, makes a big
production of signing her name all big and flowery.

"Um, we're here to discuss *me*," I remind everyone.

Ms. Weber, my math teacher, with the too much
blue smeared over her eyes, opens up her grading book.

"Victoria has been on a steady decline in mathematics this whole semester. I believe that she is heading toward a failing grade in my class for this term. I have seen no marked improvement."

"Well, I'm sure something can be done," Mom says.

"I don't like to be in a position to fail such a fine student," Ms. Weber says. "If Victoria can manage a fifty-five percent on her statewide test, I would be willing to pass her with a sixty-five percent in the class."

"But that will ruin my average," I say.

"Your average is already ruined," Dr. Gellar reminds me most unpleasantly.

I have to just face up to the fact that I'm never going to be valedictorian. I just have to let it go.

I breathe in and out, concentrating on a relaxation technique that I learned watching kung fu movies.

What's important? What's important? I say over and over to myself. *This is not a thing to get upset about. It's only math.*

I make a list of things to actually get upset about:

1. drilling for oil in the national reserves
2. war
3. the lack of water conservation
4. genetically modified foods
5. the environment
6. the melting of the polar ice caps

7. tyranny around the world

8. monoculture

"Victoria, do you have anything to say about this?"

They've been talking and talking and I haven't been listening.

"I can still go to college if I pass trig, right?"

Dr. Gellar nods yes.

"I mean, I only have to graduate, right?"

Dr. Gellar and Ms. Weber nod in agreement.

I stand up and stick out my hand to strike the fifty-five-percent deal with Ms. Weber.

"Okay, I'll take the fifty-five percent. But if I do better, then I want it weighted accordingly."

"Fair enough," Ms. Weber says. "And get a tutor."

"I'm on it," I say.

I leave the room. I push out the door and break into the sunlight and skip across the school courtyard. Today is a beautiful day. The sky is blue, because the rain has washed away all the haze. Los Angeles is most beautiful the day after it rains. I see some litter on the ground and I pick it up and throw it in the trash. I'm already making the world a better place. I head for the library and find Rue sitting there, her nose in a book.

"Rue, I know I've been just an awful person. I've been really mean and unlikable. But I need to pass math. I thought maybe we could strike a deal," I say.

Rue looks me up and down. She knows I wouldn't have come here crawling and begging unless I had something really good to offer her. I want her to see that I am a changed person.

"Okay, Victoria. I'm all ears," she says.

And I begin to reveal to her a plan for payment that I think she'll really like.

Lunchtime.

Special *Melrose Lion* Meeting.

I am alone at the end of the table at the *Lion* meeting. There are two empty chairs on either side of me. I try to ignore the fact that no one will sit next to me. Although I am making big steps with everyone else, I still can't get Max to talk to me. I just don't know how to be his friend again.

I smile a lot. I heard someone say once that it takes fewer muscles to smile than to frown, so I'm trying it out. Also, I don't want Max to know that I'm miserable. I don't want Max to know how much I realize I have to say to him. I don't want him to know that I am sorry.

"We have a winner," Ms. Dicostanzo announces to the *Lion* staff. She's in a new faux-1940s phase. Her bangs are short.

She holds up the letter from the statewide contest that Max, Nelly, and I have won.

Blah, blah, blah. Ms. Dicostanzo is talking. I can't hear her. I am a winner. It is such good news to hear, since I've felt like a loser for so long.

"So, the four of us will go to the awards ceremony together," Ms. Dicostanzo says. I am sure she already knows what dress she will wear to the ceremony.

I look over at Max and Nelly, who I can see share my pride.

"If I ever decide to go to college, this is going to look great on my application," I hear Nelly say.

Everyone on the *Lion* staff is clapping, and they are congratulating Max and Nelly. Everyone clamors around them.

I am still smiling at my end of the table, alone. Nobody comes over to congratulate me. I am still smiling, though, because I don't want anyone to know that my heart is breaking.

After what seems like an eternity, or at least a day on Jupiter, Max shoots me a look. His lips barely curl at the ends into the tiniest of smiles, and his head nods so slightly in approval I am afraid that I am imagining it. Before I can respond in kind, he looks away.

Tuesday. April 14. 4:37 P.M.
Sam Jurgen's Creature Shop.

"I'm so glad that you're back in town, Dad," I say. "I really missed you."

"I'm sorry I can't be your date to that awards dinner," Dad says. "I'm meeting with the director to go over my character sketches."

"I just don't want to go alone," I say. "Mom can't go with me either, because she's got a film premiere to go to."

"I know how important this award is to you," he says.

I realize it feels like my parents are growing up. Moving on. Getting their careers on track. Now that I'm supposed to be a young woman, they're leaving me in the dust.

"Sometimes, Victoria, the joy is in knowing how much you want to share something and learning how to enjoy it alone. Alone is different from lonely," Dad says.

176

"I understand," I say. But I want to tell him that I am lonely. That I am too good at being alone. I'm friendless and awful.

"What's this?" he asks, looking over my shoulder at my open notebook.

"What?" I say.

"These sketches?" he asks.

"Just doodles," I say.

In the margins of my class notes are my monster ideas, the doodles I do when I'm listening to the teacher but also restless with my hands. Lately I've been drawing vampires and bats, since Dad has been working on them himself. Dad starts flipping through the pages.

"Can I photocopy this page?" he asks.

He is pointing at a page where I have been drawing multiple bat wings. The wings have human arm elements in them.

"It's just a doodle, Dad," I say.

"Victoria, these are previsualization character sketches for the transformation of a vampire into a bat," he says. "It's a completely unique way of solving the transformation problem."

Dad squeezes me in a bear hug.

"Good job," he says.

I smile. I did something good.

Thursday. April 16. 6:15 P.M.
King Kong Café.

It cost me $24.13 to copy the entire Greek Mythology trilogy script. I have it in a brown manuscript box, because it's too thick to staple or bind. If my mother ever finds out that I stole her script and then replaced it next to her bed, she will disown me.

She had to sign a confidentiality agreement when she signed her contract. I don't know why. Everybody can find out what happened to all the Greek gods. They just have to read the myths for themselves.

"Do you have it?" Rue asks.

"Yeah," I say. "Here it is." I push the box over to her.

She opens the box and peers inside. She cracks a smile and pushes a latte toward me.

"I bought you a latte," she says. "Half-caf with nonfat milk. Chocolate sprinkles."

It's my favorite.

"Thanks," I say. I don't know what Rue's favorite coffee drink is, but I'm going to. That's what friends do.

She opens up the math textbook, which of course I've forgotten, and we get to work. Rue really knows what she's doing.

I bet she'll be valedictorian. Actually, I think I'm kind of rooting for her.

Friday. April 17. 2:55 P.M.
Sidewalk Outside of School.

On my way to see a double feature at the two-dollar theater, I notice a group of people. They're marching in a circle on the sidewalk just next to the school. I can't get past them; they've covered the whole sidewalk.

"What's going on?" I ask someone with a sign.

"School janitors' strike."

"Why?"

"We want a living wage."

"Why aren't you in front of the school?" I say.

"Because the district won't let us speak there. So we're speaking here so we don't get arrested."

All of a sudden, I don't think going to the movies is very important. I get my camera out of my bag and start to take pictures. I start to chant along.

Why shouldn't the school janitors get what they deserve? I sign the student petition that a hippie kid is passing around.

All these people on the sidewalk, jammed together for a real cause. Something real.

180

Wednesday. April 22. 3:12 P.M.
Melrose Lion Meeting.

Max and Nelly are deep in conversation. Ms. Dicostanzo floats into the room. Her lipstick today is a dramatic deep-black orchid. She's just had her eyebrows done. She kicks some of the papers from the wastepaper basket that have spilled over onto the floor.

"Ugh. God, this school is just a mess. And it's beginning to smell. Has anybody else noticed that?"

"That's 'cause the janitors are on strike, Ms. Dicostanzo," I say.

Max Carter looks up at me.

I push an envelope of photographs that I took at the picket line Friday after school.

"That's mine and Max's story," Nelly says.

"I didn't write a story. I took some pictures."

Ms. Dicostanzo flips through the proof sheet and the three photos I blew up to eight by ten. She nods and clucks with approval.

"This one," she holds up one of my photos. "This one goes on the cover."

She passes them over to Nelly, who doesn't pick them up.

Nelly protests. "Max is doing the cover."

Max picks up the picture that Ms. Dicostanzo likes and examines it.

"Not this time," Max says. "This should be our cover."

"No," Nelly says.

"Let's vote," Max says. "Hands up for Egg's pic being the cover."

To my surprise, every hand in the room goes up except for Nelly's.

"Fine," Nelly says. "Let's move on to other business."

4:03 P.M.
Melrose Boulevard.
I'm walking slowly down the street. I have some time to kill before I go to the Egyptian for the Sixties Science Fiction Festival.

"Hey." Max pulls on my shoulder.

I turn and face him. There is a silence between us.

"That's a great photograph," he says. "I didn't know that you were at the picket line."

"I'm full of surprises," I say. "I'm living in the real world now."

182

"I can see that," Max says.

I look straight into Max Carter's eyes.

"Friends?" I say.

"Friends," he says.

It's the best word there is, really. *Friends.*

"I gotta go. I'm late to meet my dad at the editing room. See you tomorrow, okay?"

"Of course," I say, and then watch Max Carter's retreating figure.

I think I will float to the Egyptian today. I am too happy to just walk.

Friday. April 24. 3:59 P.M.
Walking Home.

I see it while crossing the street. It is taped perilously to
the Walk/Don't Walk sign.

Protest Against GMOs
(Genetically Modified Organisms)
Demonstration—March—Costumes
Pershing Square, Downtown
Saturday, May 2nd, 12 Noon
Come Dressed as Frankenfood!!

I tear down the sign and shove it into my bag.

I am hungry, I'm sick of takeout, and I know that
the chances of there being anything good in the fridge at
home are slim. So I head into the Good Stuff natural
supermarket and I spend twenty bucks on some soba
noodles and vegetables.

In the kitchen there's a wok that my mother got from some game show she did. It has never been used. I take it out from under the sink, oil it up, and begin preparing dinner. I hear the front door squeak open and the sound of Mom kicking off the very high heels that she always wears to meetings with her agent.

"They make my legs look like they're still twenty," she always says.

She pads over to the kitchen and peers over my shoulder as I'm stirring up the veggies with some tofu and ginger soy sauce.

"I didn't know you could cook," Mom says.

"I figure if I can whip up a batch of realistic fake eyeballs, I can cook anything," I say.

Mom laughs so hard spit flies out. So I begin to laugh along with her. It feels good to laugh together.

"I never thought of it that way," she says. "I could have used that line when I was with your father. Maybe he would have cooked dinner for me once."

"There's enough for two," I say.

Mom doesn't miss a beat as she sets the table.

For once we are not going to order in and eat from the Styrofoam boxes that separate us into pad Thai and chicken piccata. For once we are not going to eat in different rooms or in front of the television because we don't have anything to say. For once we are going to eat like a family.

I dole out the portions into the seldom-used bowls, and Mom doesn't make a big deal out of it or try to force a conversation. She is just Mom. I am just Victoria.

I'm being quiet until Dad is finished working on the delicate veins in the fake bat he's making. He has used some of the elements that I came up with in the design.

I know that this silent time with Dad, when we are both working side by side, is when I have some of my happiest moments. I want to have this feeling of joy inside of me more than just on Tuesdays. I have a plan.

I open my mouth and ask for something I've never asked for before from my dad. I ask him for a real big favor. I don't know how he'll react.

Maybe he'll be mad.

"All my worldly plans are changing," I say.

"Really? How so?" he asks.

"I don't think I want to go to college right away."

"That's not a big deal. What would you do?"

"I could go to Poland with you and work on *Dracula*. You could use me as an intern. I do real good work. I learned from the best."

187

I can't read my dad's face. It's neutral, like one of his masks in a resting position. I can't tell if he's pleased or pissed that I want to come hang out and do grunt work for him.

"I learned from the best," I say again, trying to plead my case. "I want to make it my career."

"You're serious about this?" he asks.

"Yes."

"You'd have to start at the bottom. No special treatment just because you're my daughter."

"I'm ready," I say.

"It's more complicated than just saying yes," he says. But I see the wheels turning in his brain, like when he's trying to solve a problem. I know then that he's going to try to make it work.

Thursday. April 30. 6:33 P.M.
Statewide Student Journalism Awards.
Beverly Hills Hilton.

My mom's Town Car drops me off.

"I'm really sorry I can't make it," she says. "I know you're bummed."

"You gotta do what you gotta do," I say.

"I hope this isn't going to be something that you'll hold against me in therapy when you're forty, like I do with my mom."

I laugh.

"You really want to go to Poland with your dad and not to Greece with me?" Mom says.

"If I go to Greece, I'll have fun—you know, the Acropolis, Greek myths, and all. But if I go to Poland, I'll be learning something. I'll be doing something of my own."

"I know you are very talented."

"You do?"

"Oh, yes, Victoria. I'm so proud of how talented you are. I'm really happy you've found something that you like to do. Even if I find it horrifying."

"Thanks, Mom," I say. "Let me know who you find holding hands."

Mom salutes me and closes the door and goes off to Mann's Chinese Theater to the film premiere. I am glad that she's getting invited to those things. I like seeing her now on *ET* or *Access Hollywood*. I like seeing her laugh so much. I love her telling me stories about walking the red carpet.

My mom is a funny lady.

My comfort level drops, though, once her Town Car pulls away, leaving me alone at the steps of the Beverly Hills Hilton.

I head inside.

"Guest or recipient?" the woman at the registration desk asks.

"Recipient," I say.

I pull myself up to full height, posture straight. I open my evening jacket that I made myself out of some dyed fake fur and show that I am wearing a very nice outfit, a dress I created this afternoon. I let the woman know I look like a winner because I am one.

"Name?"

"Victoria Jurgen," I say.

The woman scans the guest list with her finger and then crosses my name off and hands me a badge with my name on it.

"Where's your guest? Is he or she coming later?" the woman asks.

"No," I say. "I'm here alone."

"Here's your goody bag," she says, and hands me a heavy canvas bag packed with swag from all the sponsors. Most of it is paper.

"Guess they killed a lot of trees," I say.

A man standing behind me laughs and I laugh, too. I'm not so nervous anymore.

I am Victoria Jurgen. Winner.

6:59 P.M.

Beverly Hills Hilton Grand Ballroom.

I park my jacket at the coat check and wobble over to my table. I'm not an expert at walking in heels yet. These aren't even high, but they're higher than combat boots and sneakers. I am on a higher plane. They make me walk different. I am taller, and I'm already tall.

The slip of paper the woman gave me says *Table 13.*

I scan the crowd for a familiar face. I see Max at the same moment that he sees me. He puts his napkin down and stands up as I approach the table.

"Wow," Max says. "I almost didn't recognize you."

"Is that a compliment?" I ask. I know it is. But I want him to say it.

"Hell, yeah," Max says.

My hair is growing in, and in general I am less scary looking. But I'm never going to be normal. I'm glad about that.

He moves out from behind his chair and pulls out my seat for me. I feel like a lady.

"Mom," Max says, pointing to a short spiky-haired, sharp-looking woman with big silver jewelry. "This is Victoria."

"Hi," she says. "You're a legend in the Carter household."

The Carter family laughs, but no one explains why I'm a legend.

I wonder if Nelly is as much of a legend as I am. I doubt it as I watch Nelly and her parents approach the table. Max does not get up. He does not pull out her chair. He is not sitting next to her. He stays in his seat next to me.

There is something different about Max and Nelly. Maybe they had a fight?

"Hi," Nelly says, and the inevitable introductions are made.

"Where are your parents?" Nelly asks, calling attention to the empty seat that doesn't complete our table.

"Yes, I was hoping to meet your mother," Nelly's dad says. "I had a poster of her on my wall when I was in college."

"I move alone," I say.

"The mechanas can track packs of humans," Max says, completing the line from *Terminal Earth*.

"What are you talking about?" Nelly asks, half-buttered whole-grain roll in her hand. She has to lean across the table to be included. "Are you guys speaking in comic-book code?"

"No, it's from *Terminal Earth*," I say.

"Oh, I never saw that movie," Nelly says. "When I'm an actress, I think I only want to do romantic comedies."

Max and I give each other a look.

I kick my shoes off under the table. I'm afraid I'm getting a blister from where the new shoe rubs against my foot. I listen to the ebb and flow of conversations. I'm not taking part—not because I'm isolating myself but because I'm listening.

Max makes an emphatic point to his parents about animal research, and his fork flies off the table and onto the floor. We both reach down instinctively to grab it, our heads knocking into each other. While still under the table, beneath the cloth, in our own private world, he takes his hand and touches my head where we have connected. His mouth is so close to me I could kiss it.

His eyes are holding mine. He notices my shoeless foot, and he slips the fingers of his forkless hand down under my toes and squeezes them.

"We're up," Max says as the master of ceremonies suddenly calls out our category and announces our names. We emerge from under the table to the sound of applause and are met by Nelly's angry eyes.

I don't bother putting my shoes on as we cross between the tables to the podium and receive the medal for our Garbage Art piece.

"Outstanding," Max says to me.

10:15 P.M.
The Carter Family Car.
I'm in the back seat with Max. I have my medal in my goody bag and my leg pressed up against him. Neither of us moves our bodies an inch in either direction. It is amazing how long you can go without even daring to breathe. The energy running between us makes a perfect electric current.

Mr. and Mrs. Carter's conversation becomes a hum

194

in the front seat. The light from the streetlamps occasionally highlights Max's face. I steal glances at him. I love his high cheekbones. His awkward nose. The loose strand of hair falling from his ponytail.

I feel Max stealing glances at me. When I look at the floor of the car, I notice his hand perched on the edge of his leg, which is still pressing against mine. I notice the curl of the fingers and how open they are. Welcoming. My hands are in my lap. I can see how easy it would be to put my hand in the curve his thumb and forefinger make. How easy it would be to hold his finger, or lace mine through his. I can see how fun it would be. How meaningful. But I can't seem to make the jump from my body to his.

What if he didn't hold my hand back?

Besides, he's with Nelly. Isn't he?

"This is my house," I say, breaking the silence in the back seat. After talking all night, after having so much to say to each other after not having spoken for so long, after monopolizing each other throughout the evening, in the car we didn't speak at all. "Thanks for the ride home."

"A pleasure," Flint Carter says. "And I mean it, come by the editing room anytime."

"Thanks," I say. "Bye, Max."

"Bye," Max says.

I pause for a second, waiting for something else to follow, but it doesn't. So I leave the car.

"Wait." Max runs after me. My heart jumps. Max is running toward me. Then I notice my goody bag is in his hand. "You forgot your medal."

"Brain freeze, I guess," I say.

"So you'll meet me at Pershing Square, for the Frankenfood protest?" Max says.

"Yeah, I'll look for you, and you look for me."

He stands there for a minute.

"Nelly and I are over," Max says. "I just wanted you to know."

Max shoots his head forward and kisses my cheek roughly with his slightly dry lips.

"See you," he says. He runs back to the car.

He does see me. Because I'm not invisible anymore.

In my pile of opened mail are three college acceptance envelopes.

Better news than all three of those things put together is the trigonometry exam in my back pocket with the grade of seventy percent and Ms. Weber's smiley face that says, *Well Done!*

But the most outstanding thing of all is the e-mail from my dad's travel agent with my confirmed flight itinerary for Poland.

I, Victoria Jurgen, am going to be a Vampire and Bat Wing Apprentice.

It takes a lot of yarn to make a broccoli headdress. On the flyer for the Frankenfood protest march, it said to come dressed as a genetically modified food item. I have chosen to present myself as Franken-broccoli.

This time, going downtown, I know exactly which bus to take. I hop on the number 14, glaring at everyone who stares at me with my painted green face and my broccoli statement. I look around the bus, imagining which vegetable each person looks like most. I do this by taking the lines of their face and imagining how I would extend them and mold them.

There is a tomato in the back seat, a radish by the back door, and a yellow squash next to a spinach leaf by the window. I amuse myself with this until it's my stop.

There is a large crowd of people assembling at Pershing Square. There are signs. Singing and music greet me. I begin to feel like an idiot for coming here by myself and not trying to hook up with Max earlier. I

198

wonder if I'll see him on the long walk to the convention center.

A guy with a large puppet dressed up as a corporate office drone with wads of toilet-paper dollars flowing out of its felt pockets says hello to me.

I don't see Max.

"Where do I go?" I ask a girl with rings and widening earlobe holes and more tattoos than skin.

"Oh, you look great!" she says, and points me over to the table where other demonstrators are.

There are many more people there than I imagined. I get lots of compliments on my broccoli outfit.

A horn sounds and we begin to march.

The walking is slow. The chanting is loud.

"Do we want fish genes in our spinach!"

"No!"

"Do we want frogs in our carrots?"

"No!"

As we are walking, chanting, and singing, I keep scanning the crowd for Max. But after a bit, I get over it because the protest is exciting. It's important. I am singing. I am broccoli.

We arrive at the convention center—firm, proud, together. People are giving impassioned speeches. In the distance a drum circle is beginning. There are stands of organically grown vegetables.

Hungry, I make my way over to one of the stands and get an organic veggie wrap. That's when it happens. I feel a vacuum of silence. And then drops of water begin to rain down on me. I know something bad is happening. That's when the roar begins.

"You need to clear this area," a bullhorn blares. I turn around and I see the police horses and riot gear.

"What's happening?" I ask the person next to me.

"I guess there's trouble," she says. "Better try to get out of here."

Like a distant hum, the police begin to move in, sprays of water arcing above the crowd. People are pushing to get out.

I feel paralyzed. It seems wrong to run. It seems more sane to stand my ground. Like Dad says, Document, document, document. I pull my camera out and begin snapping pictures.

I am still standing there snapping away as the people—scared, crying, wet—push by me.

"Egg!"

"Max!" I say, following him down an alley. He pushes me into a doorway. We peer out and see the crowds running by.

"What's happening?" I ask.

"Somebody threw a bunch of rotten vegetables at

some scientists entering the convention center," Max says. "The police decided to break up the protest."

"It was so strange. The silence, right before everything went haywire," I say.

Max finally takes a good look at me in my outfit and laughs. "Egg, are you in there?"

"Egg is gone. It's just me," I say. "Victoria."

The shouting just outside the alleyway begins to subside. The only sound I can hear is the beating of my heart.

"You okay?" Max asks.

"I'm a fighter," I say.

It's something that I always said because Egg said it, but now I say it because I mean it. I am a fighter.

"I think it's safe now," Max says.

We emerge into the empty, trashed remnants of the protest. I start snapping pictures. The wet, running poster board. The spoiled food. The cops.

"You can't be here, kids," a burly officer says to us. "We're clearing the area. Go home."

"I'm with the press," I say.

"Let's see some ID," he says.

Max and I pull out our *Melrose Lion* press cards and show them to him along with our student IDs.

"Freedom of the press," I say.

Max gives me the thumbs up.

The police officer turns his back to us and moves along to help another officer.

"Let's head toward the subway," I say. "We can go to Hollywood and Highland and maybe catch a movie?"

"Cool," Max says.

We head toward the nearest subway stop.

"Hey, I got into my first-choice college," Max says. "I'm going to go to the Chicago Art Institute. And I'm going to submit my graphic novel to this new comic-book company. They're looking for new stuff."

Here amongst the ruins of the day, there is still time for casual conversation. It's funny. Real life, just like in all those post-apocalyptic stories, goes on.

I put my hands to my head and feel my broccoli headdress.

"Does it still look okay?" I ask.

"Yeah, why?"

"'Cause I think it's a good design. It sure took a beating today and it's still on my head. Sturdiness is important in the movies."

Max laughs.

"What about you? What are you going to do?" he asks.

"I'm going to work with my dad on his next movie

in Poland," I say. "Then I'm coming to visit you in Chicago."

"That's what I wanted to hear," Max says.

Then his hand catches mine and I don't push it away. Instead I curl my fingers into his.

News flash:

SUN SHINES BRIGHTLY ON BRAND-NEW DAY

HOPE ABOUNDS FOR VICTORIA JURGEN

LIFE IS GOOD